THE SWORD

—— AND THE ——

IRON CURTAIN

THE SWORD

—— AND THE ——

IRON CURTAIN

By
Dr. Bo Wagner

Word of His Mouth Publishers
Mooresboro, NC

All Scripture quotations are taken from the **King James Version** of the Bible.

ISBN: 978-1-941039-53-3
Printed in the United States of America
©2025 Dr. Bo Wagner

Word of His Mouth Publishers
Mooresboro, NC
www.wordofhismouth.com

INTRO

Sergei had not returned, and everyone knew him well enough to know that that could only mean one thing.

He had been captured by the KGB.

And the KGB was very, very good at getting the information they wanted from their prisoners.

So now the church there was at risk, the church here was at risk, souls were at risk, and we Night Heroes were at risk.

But we were at risk by choice because there was no way in the world we were backing down when people had already given their lives to get these Bibles so far.

So be ready, Commies, because the Night Heroes are busting through your Iron Curtain.

And we are bringing the Sword with us.

CHAPTER ONE

"X on the exit sign..."

"No, Dad, don't do it!"

"Y right there on the Yellow Freight truck..."

"X! I see an X on that license tag!"

"Z! Z on the Jacksonville Zoo billboard!"

"Agggggh!" Aly screeched in frustration. Dad had just beaten her at the alphabet game — again—for about the billionth time in all of our travels. Somehow, it never seemed to occur to her that since he was in the driver's seat and she was in the back, he was *always* going to see all of the letters before she did.

"You'd think she'd learn by now," Carrie said flatly without even looking up from her book.

I took a sip of my tea, courtesy of our last stop at a Chick-fil-A, and just looked out the window as the palm trees whizzed by. There would be no Oklahoma Red Buds on this trip; we had just crossed over into Florida.

We, by the way, are both the Warner family and also the Night Heroes – at least us kids.

"Everybody good back there?" Mom asked from the front seat. She asked that kind of thing a lot; she was always thinking of others before herself, especially Dad and us kids.

"Not really," Aly huffed. "Dad is cheating again."

Mom just rolled her eyes and turned back toward the front.

"Awww, is my widdle bwonde hunny-bunny mad cuz she wost again?" Dad teased. Aly, the "widdle bwonde hunny-bunny," was not amused. My tiny youngest sister, age thirteen, is, well, volatile. I mean, she loves the Lord with all of her heart, and she loves all of us fiercely, but at the same time, she would also fight a grizzly bear at the drop of a hat and genuinely expect to win.

"I could use a potty break, if possible," Carrie answered.

"Yeah, ditto that," I agreed.

Dad just nodded, and I knew he would be looking for an exit with a decent place to get a splash of fuel and let everyone relieve their bladders.

I closed my eyes a bit, leaned my head back against the headrest, and smiled at how high I had to set it to do so. I enjoyed being six feet tall; not many sixteen-year-old guys are. And definitely not many are also as strong as most full-grown men. I also enjoyed this life, both being a preacher's kid and being an adventurer for the Lord.

"Hey, Genius," Dad called to the backseat, and everyone knew who he was talking to since my dark-haired, fourteen-year-old sister is indeed a genius.

"Yes, Sir?"

"Did you know that all Vikings went to heaven?"

Carrie winced.

"I hate to even ask..." she groaned. All of us knew another gem of a dad joke was coming.

"It's true," he said. "Vikings believed in reincarnation."

Carrie's eyes narrowed, and I knew she was thinking hard and fast. Aly and Dad played the alphabet game; Dad (who is also a genius) and Carrie played mind games.

"Wait, wait... ugh. Never mind. Go ahead and hit me with it."

Dad grinned out from under his mustache in the rearview mirror.

"Eventually, all of them were Bjorn again."

Mom just shook her head and sighed. The girls both stared at him like he was the corniest thing in the world. I grinned back; Bjorn again... not bad, Dad, not bad.

A few minutes later, we wheeled into a Speedway gas station, which is an okay substitute if there is not a Buc-ee's around. Dad pulled up to a pump to top off the gas, and we all tumbled out, stretched, and went inside for the restrooms and some snacks. And, since it was not a Buc-ee's, we were all back in the vehicle and heading down the road again in under ten minutes.

Every Buc-ee's stop is at least an hour long – and worth every second of it.

Anyway, after about an hour on 113 South, an hour of the bluest of blue skies, more palm trees, billboards for the Blue Angels, and clear blue water running under every bridge, we finally made the turn onto Exit 69. From there we were on Interstate 10 for about five minutes, then got off at the next exit, North Davis Highway. A minute later we were pulling into the Holiday Inn, where we would be staying for the week. Dad would be preaching at the awesome Victory Baptist Church just down the road in Milton, where Brother Tim Fellure pastors. He is one of my very favorite preachers; Dad says he is the finest orator of our day among pastors, which is a fancy way of saying that he is a really good speaker.

Four of us piled out of the Yukon and started doing luggage duty while Mom went inside and checked us in. I grabbed a luggage cart, and Carrie grabbed another. Dad and I would use maybe half a cart for our luggage, and Mom and my sisters would use a cart and a half, a few backpacks, some hands and shoulders, and maybe even a few things carried in by mouth.

Complicated critters.

We finally got checked in and loaded up, and the girls and I pushed luggage into the elevator as we and Mom headed upstairs. Dad went and parked the vehicle and then joined us in our adjoining rooms. We had been on the road for eight hours, coming from our home in the tiny town of Mooresboro, North Carolina. We were tired, wired, and in need of some rest that we were not going to get quite yet. We had an hour and a half to get to the church. And neither Mom nor Dad was okay with ever being late.

Just one of the many lessons good parents teach their children.

An hour later, we were pulling onto Avalon Boulevard in Milton. The church was on the right and was about as pretty as you might expect for a great church in Florida. And behind it was a metal building – a really important metal building. That is where Victory Baptist Press is housed. They print Bibles by the tens of thousands and send them all over the world for free.

"This church is reaching its area," Dad said as he pulled into a parking space, "but through that print shop, they are reaching the entire world. Hopefully, we will get a chance to tour it this week and see how everything works."

We opened all four doors, gathered our stuff, and headed inside. We had made it in time for the prayer room, just as Dad had hoped. Minutes later, men and boys were kneeling on chairs or on the floor, asking God for His power and presence in the service. There is nothing more important we can ever do than pray, and these people clearly knew it.

And then it was into the auditorium for service.

Pastor Fellure and his family are a lot like ours; everybody serves in the ministry along with him. His son Jacob is the assistant pastor and led the congregational singing. His other son, Parker, sang a special along with his Mom and sisters. And all of the service was an act of worship, not just some list of stuff to check off as you go.

And then, it came time for the preaching. And as many times as I have heard Dad preach, I still like it and get help from it every single time. He preached tonight from the book of Daniel on *You Can Survive The Fall.* It is a pretty cool message. Lots of people ended up falling in the book of Daniel. Three Hebrews boys were tossed like tied-up sacks of trash into a furnace. Daniel, by then a very old man, got tossed into a den of lions. And yet, all of them survived the fall. It is pretty encouraging to think that God sort of puts His giant unseen hand underneath His children in all of their "falling moments" and makes sure they land okay.

There were a lot of people around the altar during the invitation; it seems like that message hit home and helped folks.

Pastor Fellure closed the service, and we all milled around the foyer afterward for a few minutes, talking and catching up on things. And then, right as we were leaving, he asked a question that made all of us pretty excited: "Would you folks like to see the print shop tomorrow? We will be doing another run of Bibles for the foreign field, and things will be going wide open."

"Absolutely!" Dad replied with no hesitation.

"Wonderful. Then just come on over sometime tomorrow, and Brother Joseph Bertram can show you around and explain everything."

Oh, yeah!

Half an hour later, we were back at the hotel and getting ready for bed. As we do every single night of our lives, we all prayed together as a family. Then we headed to our room, our beds, our pillows, our covers...

And our very different destinations for the night.

CHAPTER TWO

One thing you should know about our Dad by now if you have read about our other adventures, is that he likes our hotel rooms to be cold. As in, "make a penguin shiver" kind of cold. And he always sets them for both rooms when we check into a hotel—meaning that if we forget to adjust ours, my sisters and I usually wake up cold.

And I was, at the moment, very, very cold. I never would have dreamed anywhere, even indoors in Florida, could be so could.

To make matters worse, while I was laying there shivering, my sisters decided to be awake and annoying; nothing is worse than having people "whisper-sing" catchy, irritating little songs to you when you are trying to sleep.

"Do you wanna build a snowman..." Carrie began.

"No. I want to sleep," I grumped.

"Or ride our bikes around the halls..." Aly joined.

15

"Stop. Just stop."

They didn't. They formed a duet.

"We think some company is overdue; we've started talking to the pictures on the walls."

And that's when it hit me. And I mean literally hit me.

"WHHHOOOOOOAAAAAA!" I shrieked. The pile of snow that had just been dumped on me let me know in an instant that we were now a very, very long way from Florida. And, I suspected, a long time away as well.

I shot straight up, gasping, while the voices of my sisters and the Conductor erupted in peals of laughter at my plight. I was so cold now that I was gasping and could not quite get any intelligible words out.

"Here, I thought you might need this," the Conductor said kindly as he tossed me a thick, heavy coat. "It has a hood, so that is a nice bonus, and there are thick gloves in the pockets."

I just nodded as I stood and started to put on those much-needed items. Other than a small lantern held by the Conductor, it was dark – very dark. We were in a sparse stand of old hardwood trees where the stars were twinkling at us through the branches. I could smell kerosene from the lamp, and I knew that was likely a clue in what was coming next.

"So, Carrie, what do you think?" he asked with a grin. We had learned pretty early on that she was a better choice than me when it came to this question.

"Got it, time and place," she said as she grinned, and I knew she had already been working all of it out in her mind.

"Obviously, there is not much to go on since we have been awakened out in the forest in the middle of the night with no landmarks in sight. But the kerosene lamp and dated clothes you have provided tell me we are probably in the 1950s or 60s. And the labels are foreign – Soviet, in fact. That, plus the fact the major constellations in the sky overhead are at a very different angle than we would be seeing them if we were still in America - "

"Wait, what?!?" Aly interrupted. "What do you mean 'if we were still in America?' "

"I mean, Sweetie, my best guess is that we are likely in Finland, not too far from the border of the U.S.S.R."

I could tell by the Conductor's nod of approval that she had nailed it.

Your guesstimate of the date is spot on, young lady; you are now in the year 1965. And you are correct about Finland as well.

"Finland?" Aly said with a hint of relief in her voice, "Well, at least it's not as far away as when we were in Germany."

Carrie grimaced and put her hands on Aly's shoulders as she looked intently into her face to get her attention.

"It's further, Sweetie. Much further. Like, 1,400 miles or so further."

"Your sister is correct, young lady. And now that Kyle is all suited up against the cold, I suggest you three get moving. Even the heavy coats and gear you are now wearing will not keep you warm out here for very long. And hypothermia is not a pleasant way to go."

"Excuse me, Sir," I said as I got my right-hand glove snugged down tight, "but exactly why are we here, and where are we supposed to go?"

He nodded again.

"Fortunately for you, I have been given a bit more to go on at the start than some other missions you have had. Your Father doesn't want you staying out here too long; He loves you too much for that."

We Night Heroes knew what Father he was talking about.

"The trail before you will weave up through this stand of trees, over the ridge, and down toward a small valley. Once you cross the ridge line, you should start seeing glimpses of a light now and then filtering through the trees. It will be from the porch lamp of a small house, or a church, depending on what day of the week it is and who is expected. Go there, knock on the door, finish the sentence, and you will be allowed to enter."

We nodded. Then we knelt.

"Father," I began, and I could feel the bitingly cold air as I inhaled before I continued, "Thank you for allowing us to serve you. We know now where and roughly when we are. We know we are heading for an underground church. And we know that these people are serious about you, way more serious than most Christians in America will ever understand. Whatever you have sent us here for, whatever help they need, please help us so that we can help them. We pray this in Jesus' name, amen."

When we rose to our feet, the Conductor was gone. I smiled as I followed his footprints in the deep snow; seven steps, and then they simply stopped, but he himself was absolutely gone.

"Wouldn't it be cool if we could just 'poof!' out of one place and into wherever else is next!" Aly said with a grin.

I pulled my coat more tightly around my neck against the ever-growing wind.

"It would, Twerp, it would. But since we don't have that option, and it is getting colder by the minute, I suggest we put the ankle express in high gear."

With no further ado, we started traipsing up the incline through a lovely stand of trees. The bright moon overhead was shining down on the snow and ice that adorned their leaves, almost giving them a twinkly Christmas tree effect.

As we crested the top of the ridge and headed for the valley below, I turned to Carrie.

"So, Finland, the Soviet Union, the underground church, what do we need to know?"

Carrie put both hands to her mouth and breathed a hot breath on them to warm them up through her mittens and then breathed out into the cold air and watched as her vaporous breath dissipated in front of her.

"World War II ended on September 2, 1945. The good guys, America and Britain and their allies, won. But the 'good guys' were not all exactly good guys. The Soviet Union, or more properly, the Union of Soviet Socialist Republics, the U.S.S.R., was on our side during that war. They used to be called Russia, and in our day, they are once again called Russia. And in a lot of ways, they were and are absolutely evil.

"After the war ended, they really pushed to expand communism around the world, especially in all of the countries in their part of the world. Naturally, the Western nations wanted to stand against that; they had just liberated the world from Nazi-ism and didn't want to see it fall to just as big of an evil as communism. But no one wanted to start another world war, either.

"So from 1946-ish to 1991, there was this thing called the Cold War instead."

"Cold war?" Aly asked with bewilderment in her voice. "Is that like a war fought only in the wintertime or something?"

"No, Sweetie, not even close," Carrie replied. I could hear the crunching of the snow under our feet for the next few seconds as Carrie gathered her thoughts for an explanation.

"The Cold War was kind of a passive-aggressive thing," she said as Aly's eyebrows raised in understanding.

Carrie continued, "There was no army versus army thing going on, but there were assassinations, spies, moles planted in other governments to destabilize things, psychological warfare, and a huge arms buildup."

Knowing what Aly was liable to ask next, Carrie beat her to it.

"No, not like Dad lifting weights; military arms: weapons, especially nuclear weapons. Nobody used them, but everybody used them as a threat. The main thing happening during the Cold War, though, was communism expanding to the nations around the USSR whether they liked it or not. Before it was all said and done, the Soviet Union, East Germany, Poland, Hungary, Albania, Yugoslavia, Bulgaria, Czechoslovakia, and Romania were enslaved under communism, among others. On the other side were nations under capitalism, sometimes called free markets. It is what we have in America, basically the ability to go where you want and buy what you want and do what you want freely. Some of them, like Finland, were in a very precarious position. They bordered the Iron Curtain countries, so they did not want to make the Communists mad enough to invade them, but they did not want to alienate the West either. They were technically neutral, but you never could tell from moment to moment whether they were going to help someone escape or send them back if they tried to escape. More often than not, they sent them back.

"As you might expect, people don't exactly want to live under slavery and tyranny. And that meant that a lot of people would try to get away and move to freedom in other countries—far, far away. But that would weaken the power of the monsters in charge, and they loved their power above all else.

"So to keep that from happening there was a metaphorical iron curtain put in place."

That one surprised even me.

"Metaphorical iron curtain?"

"Yes, Kyle, a metaphorical iron curtain. There was no way to put an actual iron curtain around tens of thousands of miles of borderland, but there were gates and fences and guards and guard towers and electronic surveillance. All of this served two primary purposes. One, to keep the people in. Two, to keep God out."

My jaw dropped; I was blown away and not quite sure I had just heard what I heard.

"You mind running the last part by me again?"

Another couple of seconds of silence passed as Carrie gathered her thoughts once again.

"We are going to need to drop a bit further back in time on that one for you to really get it. So, here goes. A long time ago, Russia was a place of beauty and freedom. There was art, culture, religion, and a proud history. But that all began to change in 1917. The government of the czars was overthrown by radical leftist revolutionaries. Five years later, in 1922, the U.S.S.R. was officially born, and one of the largest countries on Earth was about to learn what socialism and communism are all about. The Marxist revolutionaries promised a utopia, an 'equitable society.' They always do, but it never goes like they say.

"The 'father' of the new country was Vladamir Lenin. But as bad as he was, the next man in charge, Joseph Stalin, was infinitely worse. By the end of the decade, he was the supreme dictator. Along the way, he and his minions established atheism as the state religion. The government itself founded the League Of Militant Atheists to help stamp out any belief in God. People were persecuted horribly, stigmatized, ruined if they were found to be believers."

"Whoa..." Aly whispered.

"Yeah, 'whoa' indeed," Carrie answered. "Stalin eventually died, but that policy continued. For a long time, the government tried to embarrass Christianity out of existence. But since that did not work as well as they hoped, they tried literally killing it. Believers were prone to have secret services in houses, hoping the government would not find out about them. But officials had eyes and informants everywhere, and time and again, soldiers would kick the doors in, beat people, leaving many dead and many wishing they were dead. And at the border, guards made sure that no Bible ever, EVER made it into their territories. They knew that, in the words of Jesus, 'ye shall know the truth, and the truth shall make you free,' and they were not interested in anyone having any kind of freedom.

"Seeing all of this developing, Sir Winston Churchill gave a speech in which he said, 'From Stettin in the Baltic to Trieste in the Adriatic, an iron curtain has descended across the continent.'"

"From then on, these nations enslaved in communism were referred to as being behind the Iron Curtain. They would live and die under tyranny, and most of them would also die lost since the gospel and the Word of God were kept from them."

At that moment, Aly piped up, "The light!"

"Right, Sis," Carrie answered, "they would never get to see the light."

"No," Aly said more forcefully, "the light!" She was pointing as she said that, and as we followed her arm, I could just barely see the light from the porch and window twinkling through the icy branches that were swaying lightly in the breeze.

CHAPTER THREE

As we drew nearer and nearer to the little house and the light source coming from it, my stomach began to tense up. We were absolute strangers about to approach people whose lives were constantly at risk and, therefore, they would not be inclined to trust us at all. Worse still, we did not yet have any idea why we were doing so.

"What did he mean by 'finish the sentence, and you will be allowed to enter'?"

I looked down at my intense littlest sister and smiled.

"I'm not sure, Pipsqueak. I suspect this will be some kind of a code that will either mark us as okay if we know it or as big trouble if we don't."

"Well, that could be a problem," she said as she wrinkled up her face. "Exactly what sentence are we supposed to finish? He didn't give us that seemingly important bit of information."

I just shrugged. "I have no idea. I just know God would never send us into anything unless He has already equipped us for it. So what say we just take it one step at a time and trust Him?"

She nodded, satisfied.

A moment later, our six snowy boots tromped up three wooden stairs onto an old wooden porch. I could smell the smoke from the chimney rising into the night, and I knew it would be the only source of heat for those inside.

Tentatively, I knocked on the door. Even out here in the middle of the woods in the middle of the night, it just seemed like quiet was the way to go.

Footsteps shuffled toward the door, and then a voice said:

"Juu?"

Aly and I both looked over at Carrie, who hissed, "No, I do not happen to know Finnish."

Apparently, the voice inside heard her say that.

"American?"

"Yes," I quickly answered, "we are American."

Several seconds of silence followed. And then the voice replied again:

"Behold, I stand at the door and knock."

I smiled and picked it up from there.

"If any man hear my voice, and open the door, I will come in to him, and will sup with him, and he with me."

Light quickly spilled out of an ever-widening crack in the door until the door itself was wide open, and we were standing face-to-face with a round, bespectacled little man. A look of shock quickly filled his face.

"What are three children from half a world away doing here, in the middle of the night, in the dead of winter? Come in, quickly, before you freeze to death!"

Gratefully, we did just that.

It took mere seconds for our eyes to take in the entire tiny scene. This one-room cabin in the woods was no bigger than the average living room in an American house of our day. Besides us, there were twelve people inside: six ladies, two men, and four children. Each one had a Bible – and little else.

As the door closed behind us, I could see both fear and confusion on everyone's faces. Visitors were clearly a dangerous thing at a time when the authorities in that part of the world were trying to find and root out Christians, even those technically outside of the Iron Curtain. But the fact that we were Americans is what brought on the confusion that seemed to be bigger than the fear at that moment.

"I asked you a question," the round man replied as he squared up to face us once again. "What in the world are you doing here? I suspect you to be believers, based on your ability to so easily finish that Scripture verse. But one cannot be too sure, or too careful in these parts. So again, why are you here, and who are you?"

I substantially towered over this man, but he showed absolutely no fear whatsoever. I grinned, already knowing the answer to the question/statement I was about to ask.

"I assume you are the pastor, sir?"

His mouth said nothing; his face said nothing either. So I continued.

"We are the Warner children; we are from America, and we are most definitely believers. Our father is an evangelist, a preacher of the gospel."

Then I hesitated for just a second. This was always the tricky part...

"Our father is preaching a meeting, and we always travel with him and try to serve the Lord as he does. He cannot be here right now, and I cannot explain why; we also have secrets that need to be kept in order to keep everyone that we love safe. But what you really need to know is that God sent us here and that we are willing to give our very lives, if necessary, to help with whatever your need is. You do not know us, but please trust me when I tell you that there is more to us than meets the eye. If God has sent us here, there is a reason, probably a big one. So, please let me turn the tables just a moment and ask you a question: what exactly is going on in this precious, underground church? What has happened, and what do you need? In short, why don't you please tell us why we are here?"

Hours had passed. Roughly half of the people had slipped out into the night to trudge to their homes before daylight before anyone could realize they had been gone worshipping the Lord. The others were still there, curled up on the floor around the fireplace. Aly was sound asleep along with them.

"So, how long have you been doing this?" I asked the pastor.

"The smuggling operation has been going on for a few years now. It started small but has grown to quite an extensive network. We have a print shop in the basement of a bakery in the village just a few miles to the south. Once the Bibles are printed and ready, they are brought here, stored in the cellar, and then, box by box, smuggled across the border. The underground church there in the U.S.S.R. then distributes them to people who need them. Thus far, God has protected our people magnificently; none have been lost. But Sergei is overdue, and he is our very best. He has never been late returning before."

I mused on that in quietness for a few moments. During the previous hours, the pastor had told me about all of his wonderful people. He had spoken at length, though, about Sergei. This wonderful brother had been saved as a young man under his ministry and had given up a chance at a lucrative career in the West in order to stay and smuggle the Bible past the Iron Curtain into the Soviet Union. He was smart, loyal, and godly. He was not one who would turn to the other side nor one who would get careless in his duty.

I did not say it out loud, but I was now as worried as the pastor over this. Hopefully, he was merely late due to some innocent, unforeseen circumstance. Hopefully, by tomorrow, he would return safely.

Hopefully.

CHAPTER FOUR

I could tell by the fact that I was hot and throwing covers off of me, we were no longer in Finland. The humming of the air conditioner and my sisters stirring in their bed confirmed that for me. I stretched, yawned, and thought once again about how odd it was that we could walk out of a cabin in Finland in the middle of the night, walk off into the woods, curl up together by a tree and go to sleep, and wake up in our own time many decades later.

Pretty cool life, that.

I sat up and swung my feet over the edge of the bed. A big yawn and a stretch or two, and I was heading for the bathroom. It wasn't often I got in there before my sisters, but it was always nice when I did; if not, I always had to wait a pretty long time.

As I looked in the mirror and brushed my teeth, I grinned a little bit as I paid attention to my muscles. With any luck, I may get to use them to pound a Commie or two if it comes down to that.

Nazis, Communists, I don't like anybody who keeps people in bondage.

After a few minutes, I was done and dressed and left the bathroom for the girls, who by then were up and around. And within the hour, we were all downstairs in the trusty old Yukon, heading out for a bite of breakfast. Mom and Dad's newest craze for breakfast was Dunkin' Donuts. Not for doughnuts; Mom and Dad mostly avoid sugar. But they had found that there were also pretty cool breakfast sandwiches there to go along with Mom's coffee and Dad's unsweet tea.

We didn't mind; the girls all got froufrou coffees, I got a sweet tea, and we three kids got doughnuts to go along with our croissants. And then it was off for our first adventure of the day, the print shop of Victory Baptist Press. We quickly made our way there, pulled into the parking lot, and drove around behind the church to the print shop.

As we piled out of the Yukon, Aly asked, "What do they do here?"

"On, not much, Sweetie," Dad said, "they just throw a lifeline to every drowning soul in the entire world from this single building."

Aly scrunched up her face and shrugged her shoulders, not sure exactly what that meant. I knew, and I knew that she would know before the morning was done.

As we opened the door and entered the building, we saw paper. And please get the idea of a few sheets of notebook paper out of your head, I mean PAPER. Mountains of it. I couldn't help but take a picture:

"Whoa..." Aly whispered. I looked down at her, and she was looking up at those monstrous paper rolls.

Dad started to say something, but before he could, Aly blurted out, "It's like rolls of toilet paper for Goliath!"

We all lost it, but we were not the only ones; beside us, I could hear another voice in peals of laughter, and I turned to see the friendliest-looking guy joining in our amusement over Aly's less-than-dignified evaluation.

When we all got ourselves composed, he stuck out his hand to my dad and said, "I'm glad you all got to come, Preacher. I really enjoyed the message last night. I'm Joseph Bertram, and I'll be showing you around today and explaining everything we do here.

All of us shook his hand in turns, and then the tour was off and running. "First off," he said as he pointed to the rolls of paper, "even Goliath would have a hard time handling one of these; each roll weighs about 1,500 pounds."

Now it was my turn to "Whoa..."

"Yeah, whoa," Carrie chimed in agreement.

"This big machine beside it is obviously the printing press. At the speed that we can run it, we can turn a tractor-trailer load of these paper rolls completely into Bibles in about four months. And we don't just print in English; we have done twenty languages or so, sent them to forty different countries, and we are getting ready to flood the country of Suriname with the Word of God."

"Where's Suriname?" Aly whispered to Carrie.

"About 2,700 miles that way," Carrie answered as she pointed to what I knew was southeast.

Brother Bertram continued walking and talking, and soon, we came to a piece of equipment that was really cool and really old:

"This is our Heidelberg windmill press. It is the machine that stamps our covers. It's a 1950s model, and yet it's probably our finest piece of equipment."

That was definitely a wow moment. That thing should have been in a museum, but instead, it was still helping to churn out the Word of God for an entire world.

"It's pretty amazing to think that when this thing was in its prime, Bibles that came off of it would have to be smuggled into a lot of countries, but now, we can circulate them freely in most nations of the world."

There was so much to see in the print shop. But what really caught Dad's attention was an unusual picture on the wall:

"Check the dots? There has got to be something to that..."

Brother Bertram smiled. "There is, Sir, there is. The backs of each section have dots on them so that when we look at them, we know which direction is up and which direction is down. That keeps us from making a Bible where, say, Psalms is upside down. It's a pretty good metaphor for the Christian life, though, isn't it? If all the dots of our lives line up right with the Word of God, we turn out okay, but if not, parts of our life are upside down!"

We hung out in the print shop for another hour or so, getting the explanation for everything. And then it was off for our midday adventure, otherwise known as lunch. We went to the La Hacienda Mexican Restaurant, and boy, was it good! Do you want to know why Mexican restaurants are taking over the world?

It's us, the Warners; we eat at them multiple times a week.

You're welcome.

Anyway, after an awesome lunch of fajitas, chips and salsa, quesadillas, and other south of the border delights, we headed down to Pensacola Beach. Dad always says that the beach is his happy place, and all of us Warners concurred with that view. We took a long walk, took a bunch of pictures, and collected some really cool shells. Then we came back to where we started and just sat on a blanket for a while and watched the tide roll in.

But the tide was not the only thing rolling in.

"Storm clouds," Dad said simply. Mom nodded, and all of us got up and gathered our stuff. By the time we made it back to the Yukon, the sky was getting decidedly darker, and by the time we got back to the hotel, it was pouring rain.

An hour later, we were dressed and out the door and heading back to Victory Baptist Church. We had dinner in the fellowship hall with everyone, and some of our dearest friends, the Morrison family, also known as The Morrison Sisters gospel singing group, had made it in by that time. They would be providing much of the special singing for the rest of the meeting.

It was a noisy, happy time all during supper. But finally, it was time to put everything away and head for the prayer rooms. The service would be starting soon, and people would be praying for God's presence in the meeting.

And He graciously gave it to us. Dad preached a message titled *A Difficult Day at the Potter's House.* In Jeremiah 18, a potter was trying to do his job and ended up messing up the vessel that he was working on. And it was a bad time for him; the Babylonians were heading that way to overthrow the city, and Jeremiah, public enemy number one, was just sitting there watching as he worked. But instead of quitting when things went bad, the potter started over again and made another vessel out of the clay. Because of that, nearly 2,600 years later, we are still singing songs like "He Didn't Throw The Clay Away." We are still getting help because one guy didn't quit, and God put it in Scripture for us as a picture of how He is the Potter, and we are the clay.

Lots of people came to the altar during the invitation; it seemed like the message really hit home for folks.

We hung around for a while afterward, talking and fellowshipping, and I got to talk for a while to some great guys of the church not too much older than me: Jordan Seely and the pastor's son, Parker. The girls were all talking to friends of their own.

Finally, though, Dad got us all loaded up into the vehicle and headed for the hotel.

Or to the threshold of the Iron Curtain, as the case may be.

CHAPTER FIVE

"The Conductor could have arranged for us to wake up much closer to the house so we wouldn't be freezing our patooties off," Aly grumped as we made tracks in the snow. It was deeper tonight than last night; it had clearly snowed again since we were here yesterday.

"Less moaning, more moving, Twerp," I said as I rubbed my gloved hands together for warmth.

For the next few moments, Aly contented herself with mumble-grumbling under her breath. Carrie was utterly quiet as we walked, which I knew meant that she was thinking.

"What's going through your big brain, Carrie?"

She put her hands to her mouth and blew some hot air on them and then took another step or two in silence before speaking.

"I guess I'm just thinking about the contrasts of life," she said contemplatively. I remained silent; I knew her well enough to know she would tell me what she meant.

"The warmth of Florida, the freezing cold of Finland. The conveniences of the modern day, the struggling-just-to-survive of people in this day. The freedom of America, the bondage of the Iron Curtain. It just seems like nothing is ever truly quiet even."

I mused on that for a moment and then smiled as a thought came to me.

"Do you remember when our pastor was preaching through the book of the Revelation? He talked about the time during the Tribulation Period when God will stop all of the wind on Earth. He said that if nature or science rather than God were behind it, the only way that could ever happen was for Earth to be a hyper-frozen rock, with everywhere on the entire planet the exact same temperature."

Carrie's brow was wrinkled. "What's your point?"

"Just that variety seems to be a much bigger blessing than absolute uniformity."

Aly's eyes got wide, and her mouth dropped open a bit before she finally spoke.

"Bruh, that is deep. You're like a philanthropist!"

Carrie closed her eyes and sucked in her breath as if in deep pain.

"Philosopher, Sweetie, I think you mean philosopher."

Aly just shrugged and kept walking.

"That is pretty deep, though, Kyle," Carrie said with begrudging admiration.

"Well, like Papa says, even a blind squirrel finds an acorn every now and then."

Carrie just smiled, and we kept trudging through the snow. We weren't worried about getting lost; we had gotten pretty good at keeping our bearings and finding our way around through the course of our various adventures.

Presently, the little house came into view. The sun was just now peaking over the trees and kissing the world for a brand new day of light. We hastened our pace just a bit and pretty quickly made our way up onto the porch.

I was getting ready to knock when the door abruptly swung open.

I could tell by the stony look on the pastor's face and the red, teary eyes from all of the ladies that the news was not going to be good on this day.

"Come in, Warner children," the pastor said in a strained voice, "It will not do for anyone to see you outside of this house – especially not now."

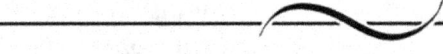

An hour had passed – an hour in which we Night Heroes mostly sat silent and listened.

"So, how did you find out?" I finally asked.

The Pastor took a deep sip of his very strong coffee, set the cup down on a rickety little side table, and said, "Even in the devil's camp, God has His angels. Some of the KGB agents have come to know Christ through the years through the efforts of other believers. Many have been found out and either sent to gulags or killed. But a few have managed to stay in their positions without being exposed. It is dangerous, but from time to time, they are able to slip information out to the churches. Such is the case here. We have no reason to doubt them, both because they have always been trustworthy and because Sergei is never late. And now, both he and the churches here and there, and the next boxes of Scriptures we have ready to smuggle in, are at risk. We will all likely be exposed and taken, and none of us will ever be heard from again. As for Sergei, they will torture him for the information and then kill him when they can get no more out of him."

I nodded, then asked, "Where is he likely to be held? And where is the shipment of Bibles supposed to go?"

I could feel Carrie and Aly staring at me. I knew that they knew what I was thinking. I also knew that in her head, Carrie was screaming, *"We need a plan! A very good and very careful plan!"* and that in her head, Aly was grinning from ear to ear and thinking, *"Let's rush in and whack absolutely everybody!"*

The pastor seemed to know where I was heading with those questions, and he tried his best to squash my thoughts immediately.

"No. Absolutely not. You are children and not even from here. You would be captured yourselves, and make matters infinitely worse, and leave me with your blood on my hands. I forbid it."

There was a moment of silence. Finally, I stood up. I had been praying silently and felt sure that I knew what I was supposed to do. I had never tried it, but I was pretty confident. Above all, I knew enough to trust the leading of the Holy Spirit.

I took a few strides toward the old wooden table in the center of the room. As I approached it, I jumped, rared my arm back, shouted, and brought my fist down with every ounce of my power right into the middle of the table.

It shattered like a pile of matchsticks.

I turned and looked at the faces of everyone in the room. On most, there was a wide-eyed, stunned silence. The pastor, though, had the faintest smile on his face and was almost imperceptibly nodding his head.

"So. God has made you strong, young man. But are you wise? And can you face overwhelming odds with courage?"

"Sir," I replied, "those words do not describe me. But they do describe US, the three of us Warner kids. None of us alone could ever be equipped for any task, let alone any task so great as this. But together, in the power of God, we are unstoppable. We will get your Bibles to the church in Russia, and if he is still alive, we will find and rescue Sergei."

He nodded. "Then there is not a moment to lose. Here is everything I know to tell you."

For the next hour or so, Pastor Virtanen told us everything about the territory between here and the border of the U.S.S.R., what he knew about the checkpoints leading in and out, and where his informants thought Sergei was being held. And then, at our request, he provided us with three backpacks much larger than the small night packs we always carried with us. Our plan was to load the Bibles into plastic bags to keep them dry within those packs, carry them to just shy of the border on this day, stow them away, and cross the Iron Curtain with them tomorrow. We knew time was limited, and not just because we were on day two of our standard five days that we always had to accomplish a mission; it was also limited because Sergei was doubtless going through a lot of pain right now, and we needed to get to him as quickly as we could, for his good and the good of the churches he could be forced to betray.

With all of our packs filled to capacity with Bibles, we strapped our small packs onto the outside of those. One of the ladies looked at Aly a bit sympathetically and more than a bit skeptically.

"Voitko kantaa sita kaikkea?"

Aly looked up at her, obviously having no clue what she said, and then looked over to the Pastor.

"She wants to know if you can really carry all of that, little one."

I could see Aly's face getting hard and red, and I knew that within about three seconds, she would be hot enough to melt all of the snow in Finland if I did not step in.

"Tell her we said thank you for her concern, but I assure you, both of my sisters are way above average; I would trust either of them with my life. She can handle the weight and then some."

We snugged everything down tight, and then the pastor pulled us into a circle and had everyone gathered around us. "Lord," he began to pray in his thick accent, "You who sent little David to Israel in their hour of greatest need, we must trust that You have likewise sent these precious young people to us in our hour of greatest need. Give them strength for the journey, sight beyond their sight, and above all, Your hand of protection. Roll back the forces of darkness and pierce the very heart of Satan himself with the Sword these young people are carrying into his territory. We pray this in the name above all names, Jesus the Christ, amen."

We all lifted our hands and opened our eyes. The pastor smiled and said, "Godspeed, young warriors, godspeed."

We nodded, shook his hand, and turned to go.

From the information the pastor gave us, we knew that we were about eight miles from the border. Normally, we could cover eight miles in a matter of two or three hours. But in the snow and carrying packs full of Bibles, we would be pushing it to make it to the border and find a safe place to hide the Bibles by nightfall.

"Let's start out at a pretty decent clip," I said, "but definitely not a run. We are going to have to keep to the trees for the most part to avoid any prying eyes that may rat us out. We need to make sure we have enough energy for the task."

"No biggie, bro," Aly chirped happily. "We are walking in a winter wonderland, and I have Starbursts. Sugar high for everybody!" she said as she tossed Carrie and me a piece of our own.

As we walked, the snow seemed to act as a blanket, muffling the sound of our steps. I thought it was kind of sad that people in this part of the world see such amazing beauty straight from the hand of our good Creator and yet choose to live in the darkness and mystery of atheism.

"Hey," Carrie said as she came up beside me.

"Yeah, whatcha need, Sis?"

"Do you think it is enough to make a difference? I mean, we are risking our lives to bring just three packs of Bibles into one of the biggest nations on earth. If we were smuggling in a tractor-trailer load of them, it seems like it would make sense. But this? This seems like a very small drop in a very big bucket."

"Maybe," I said, "but a little ball of uranium is just a drop in the bucket as well, and it has enough power to either level cities or energize cities. The people that get these Bibles will study them and memorize them and pass them around, and they will change the lives of everyone who honestly reads them; if we were only carrying a single Bible in, it would still be worth the effort."

Carrie nodded, and we kept trudging on. In a way, it felt a lot like walking through the woods back home. They were mostly pine, with some spruce and birch and elm and other trees as well, stuff that we were pretty well familiar with.

After a few hours, I could tell the girls were getting a bit tired.

"Let's drop our packs and have a quick bite of lunch, okay?"

I got no argument from them on that. There was a decent-sized conifer beside the path we had been traveling, and its branches were high up enough that it had shielded the ground beneath it from the snow. We pretty quickly set up lunch underneath it and talked and ate and rested for a while.

The area was lovely, and even in this, the dead of winter, I could see some pretty little redheaded birds hopping around in the snow, taking something they were finding to eat.

"So," Carrie said after she gulped down a bite, "what's the grand master plan here?"

"Well, you all know the plan for today. We get close enough to see the border and scout a way across, stash the Bibles in a safe place, and head for our time. Then we pray for the Lord to bring us right back to the spot where the Bibles are, cross over good and early tomorrow, get them to the church on the other side of the border, rescue Sergei, and get him home. Now, can we do it all in one day? Prooooooobably not. But I intend to get as much of it done as possible."

That seemed to satisfy her, and we all ate in silence for a few more minutes. And then, as if we had all heard the same unspoken voice, we packed our trash up, hoisted and buckled our packs, and started off for the border one more time. Based on my estimation of how far we had come, we should make it to the border with plenty of time to spare.

And I was pretty convinced of that right up until we broke out into a clearing and saw the old peat bog stretching out in front of us.

CHAPTER SIX

"Well, this is unfortunate," Carrie said dryly.

I did not respond; I was trying to take it all in. There, stretched out in front of us, was a potentially huge problem.

Peat bogs are a kind of wetland. They are actually pretty common around the world, though most American kids have likely never seen one. They are waterlogged areas of ground with a lack of oxygen in the soil, which results in slower decomposition of organic material. Because of that, peat, in this case, sphagnum moss, grows pretty rapidly in that environment. And in this area of the world, it was often mined for energy production, resulting in a bog like the one that was in front of us, which would certainly have dangerous sinkholes that we might not recognize until we were out into them, especially with pockets of snow mixed in with the peat.

"You know how dangerous that is, right?" Carrie asked.

"Yeah, Carrie, I do," I said with mild annoyance. "But look at the width of that thing; if we try to go around it, it's going to set us way back. We'll have to be careful, but I think we should try and go through."

Typically, Aly immediately bolted forward, and I snatched her by the back of her jacket.

"Whooooaaa, Lightning, easy there. I think you missed that part about 'careful.' Be still for a minute."

I looked around and pretty quickly found a reasonably-sized stick that I could poke ahead of us with.

"Okay, everyone, follow me, and watch every step you take."

If this worked, we would be well on track and well on time. If it didn't... well, I really didn't want to think about that.

The ground was mushy but not too bad. In a way, it was almost pleasant walking across the sphagnum moss; it almost felt a little bit like God's carpet. As we walked, here and there we saw stunted trees; they were surviving, but they would never thrive in such an environment. Without enough oxygen, most things never do. I thought there was probably some interesting lesson in that, something that Dad could use as a sermon illustration, but at the moment, it escaped me.

We walked on for a little way, and I was being very careful to poke ahead of me; I didn't want my sisters getting into any unnecessary danger.

"It's kind of icky," Aly said with a wrinkled-up nose.

"Definitely not gonna argue with that," Carrie replied.

"Focus, people," I said firmly. "We can't afford any mistakes. Just keep following me step for step and..."

"And?" Carrie asked from close behind me.

"And we have a problem."

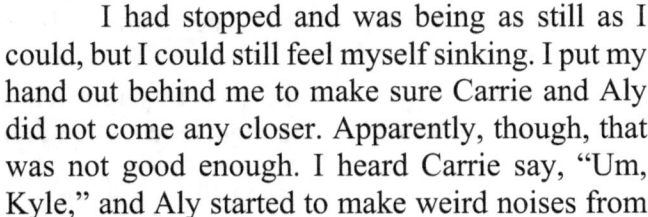

I had stopped and was being as still as I could, but I could still feel myself sinking. I put my hand out behind me to make sure Carrie and Aly did not come any closer. Apparently, though, that was not good enough. I heard Carrie say, "Um, Kyle," and Aly started to make weird noises from behind me.

"Are both of you sinking too?" I said as I turned my head around in that direction.

"Yes. Yes, we are." Carrie said in a rather professorial tone.

"Okay, just be as still as you can, and let me think for a minute."

"Could you maybe like, think quick or something?"

"Thank you for that suggestion, littlest sister; I wouldn't have thought of that."

"Now probably isn't the time for sarcasm or arguing," Carrie said coldly.

I was starting to get a little bit nervous; I had no way of knowing how deep of a sinkhole we were in or whether or not our feet would hit the bottom before our noses went under the mud.

"I can't lift my feet!" Aly yelped, and I could hear the panic in her voice.

"Be still!" Carrie shouted. "Struggling will make you sink faster. Kyle, we really need to do something!"

"I know, sis, I know. I just don't know what yet."

And that is when a fourth voice joined our conversation, a deep male voice with a thick accent.

"If I were you, I would start by removing those heavy packs and letting them sink so that you don't."

CHAPTER SEVEN

As much as I could, I twisted myself around to see the voice. We all did. And as we did, all of us knew that we now had yet another problem to deal with; it really does pour when it rains, it seems. We were looking at a large, bearded, grizzled man – and also looking down the barrel of the mean-looking weapon he was pointing at us, a weapon that I recognized as an AK-47.

"I said, If I were you, I would start by removing those heavy packs and letting them sink so that you don't."

The man's eyes were a piercing pale blue and utterly emotionless. I judged him to be about fifty years old, though with the hard life people tended to live in this part of the world, he very well could have been much younger than that.

"We can't do that, sir," I said as respectfully as I could. "We have precious items in these packs, and we have promised to get them across the border."

"Precious items, eh? Maybe I could make a few rubles off of them. Maybe I just shoot all three of you and take your packs."

"Well now," Carrie replied, "that would require you coming out here to get them, now wouldn't it?"

We were still slowly sinking, and Carrie was about to get into a battle of wits with a gun-toting stranger. Great. Just great.

The man smiled just a tiny bit. "I like this one; she has spirit. My little Anna was like that." And with that, the man put down his gun, took his own small pack off of his back, and pulled a rope out of it. "Who wants to be pulled out first while the others continue to sink?" He asked flatly. Immediately, I raised my hand while the two girls pointed at me; the man looked utterly bewildered.

"This is an easy and logical choice for us," I said with a smile. "If you pull one of the girls out first, you may grab her and try to take her away. We do not know you, so we cannot yet afford to trust you. But if you pull me out first, I will get the girls out with or without you, and I will keep them safe even if it means having to wrap that gun around your head."

The man smiled from ear to ear and laughed a deep, genuine, pleasant laugh. "I do not know your parents, but they have done a good job raising smart and brave children. Here, catch."

He tossed me the rope, and I wrapped it around my right forearm and held it tightly with both hands. The man began to pull, and in a moment or two, I was free of the sinkhole. A couple of minutes later, Carrie and Aly were both free, and we were standing on semi-solid ground with our rescuer.

I looked the man in the eyes; we were the same height. "Thank you, sir," I said sincerely. "We very much appreciate your help. May I ask whom we have had the pleasure of meeting on this day?"

"Alekhin," he said. "And since we are asking questions, may I ask what brings three American children into the middle of this godforsaken land? And what is so valuable in those packs that you would die for it?"

I smiled. "The answer to your first question is found in the second."

The man's grizzled face wrinkled up; he clearly did not know what I was getting at.

"You called this a godforsaken land. You are wrong, Alekhin. This land may have forsaken God, along with many other lands in this atheistic part of the world, but God has not forsaken this land at all. These packs we are willing to die for contain love letters from Him to you – all of you."

His face remained blank. He still did not understand, but he was listening intently.

"Carrie, turn around so I can get to your pack."

Carrie smiled and turned, and even without asking, I knew that she and Aly were both praying. I reached into her pack, pulled out a Bible, and handed it to our new friend. His eyes got really wide; I knew what was coming next.

"Pyha Raamattu," he said breathlessly. "Bible. I have not seen one of these since..."

His voice trailed off, and I was sure I was seeing the beginning of tiny tears welling up in the corner of his eyes.

Carrie nailed it, first guess.

"Anna? Was she your daughter? Was she a believer?"

There was a few seconds of silence as the man held that Bible in slightly trembling hands. Finally, he answered.

"Yes, and yes. Her mother taught her to believe in this, how do you say, Jesus? She taught her to love the Book. I wanted none of it. I scoffed, I mocked, I even blasphemed. I will never forgive myself; I can still see the hurt on her tiny face."

"How old was she, and what happened?" Aly asked tenderly. As she did, she stepped up to the man and put her hand on his hands. He jerked just a bit as if in shock, then softened and smiled.

"She was ten. She had a little round face like an angel and dark and sparkly eyes like the night, just like her mother.

"She got sick, so very sick. We went to the doctors, but they could do nothing. She wasted away day by day. And all the while, she talked about God and Heaven. In some of her moments of delirium, she would describe it as if already seeing it.

"On the day she died, she was clear-minded. She took my hands. 'Papa,' she said, 'promise me two things. Promise me that you will keep my Bible and read it. And promise me you will join me in Heaven one day.'

She died a few hours later. I knew what I had promised her, yet I buried her Bible with her. I did not want to ever see one again, nor did I ever want to see a God who would cause me such pain."

"Alekhin," I said softly, "Do you think it is an accident God sent you our way today? What are the odds you would find three American kids sinking in the peat bog, carrying the Book? Your Anna has been in Heaven and has doubtless personally been asking Jesus to send someone to you. And He did. He sent us with the Book to replace the one you buried. He sent us to remind you that God has never forsaken you; He has been right here all along, keeping you safe until we could get here with the message."

I put my hand on his shoulder.

"Friend, you did something for us. You saved our lives. May I, in return, do something for you? May I save your life, forever?"

Over the next few minutes, I got to do one of my very favorite things. While Carrie and Aly knelt and cried and prayed, I took my own Bible and showed Alekhin how to repent of his sin and trust Jesus as his Lord and Savior. Soon, he was bowing in the snow and weeping as Jesus came into his heart. Finally, he stood, raised his hands and his face to Heaven, and shouted with all of his might.

"Anna! Your prayers have been heard! Tell your mother I will see you both as soon as I am finished here!"

The woods echoed; I suspect the mansions on the streets of gold did as well.

We cried; we shouted with him; we hugged; it was epic.

Finally, though, I had to bust it all up; the day was fading fast, and we still needed to get to the border. In that, Alekhin proved to be much more than just a new friend; he proved to be a brand new fellow laborer, as the Apostle Paul would have put it. He knew every inch of the peat bog and led us safely through. He had lived in the wilderness for years now, as did many who simply wished to be left alone, especially by the prying eyes of corrupt government.

Once safely through, we prayed together, and then we Night Heroes watched as our new brother vanished back into the forest. We knew we would probably never see him again in this lifetime.

We also knew we would see him forever later on.

An hour later, we were within walking distance of the border but still far enough away to be out of sight of whoever may be watching. We carefully stowed our packs of precious Bibles, bedded down under the low-slung branches of an evergreen, and prayed for Alekhin once again and for God to bring us safely back to this spot tomorrow.

And then we went to sleep, very tired but very happy.

CHAPTER EIGHT

To shiver to sleep at night in Finland and then wake up with the warmth of the Florida sun to start your day is pretty wild. I lay there in bed for a while just thinking of our adventure so far – but also thinking that my mouth felt nasty, and I needed to get up and brush my teeth.

Aly and Carrie were still out cold in their bed as I passed by, and I am pretty sure Aly was drooling.

As I looked at myself in the bathroom mirror, I grinned; I am having to shave now, which is pretty cool. It is just fuzz, mostly, but I am apparently going to follow in Dad's 'stache legacy, or maybe even a full beard one day.

A few minutes later, I was ready for the day, and the girls were taking their (very long) turns in the bathroom.

Finally, we kids and Mom and Dad were heading down to breakfast in the lobby. The Holiday Inn there on North Davis Highway has a really sweet staff and a really good breakfast. We downed eggs, bacon, fruit, and oatmeal, along with a few extra pancakes for me.

"Hungry?" Mom said incredulously as she looked at my fourth plate.

"He's trying to grow his tiny muscles, Honey," Dad said with a grin.

I did a flex pose, Dad did one back, and immediately, we were grunting and posing at each other as if in a manhood contest.

"Good grief," or some version of that sentiment, came from all of the Warner ladies until Dad and I finally felt as if the world was duly impressed and we could safely move on to other things.

"Other things," on this day, would start with a cool thing over at the church. Several church youth groups were coming together for a quarterly Masterclubs meeting. Several young men would preach and then would be graded on how well they did.

We piled into the trusty old Yukon and headed out into the lovely Florida sun. The palms were swaying in the soft breeze, and the puffy clouds overhead seemed happy as we made our way down the highway underneath them. Twenty minutes later, we pulled into the parking lot at the Victory Baptist Church. Several vans and buses were there, as well as a bunch of cars.

Dad parked, and we piled out and went inside, sitting near the back, as always. Pastor Fellure greeted everyone cheerfully; his son, Jacob, led us in singing Crown Him Lord Of All, and then it was down to business. One by one, boys and young men were called up and given a five-minute time slot to preach. And man, let me tell you, all of them were really good! One, though, stuck out in particular to all of us: a great kid named Major Booth. He looked really sharp in a blue suit, crisp white shirt, and striped tie.

He had everyone open their Bibles to Mark 4 and read the account of the disciples in the storm on the Sea of Galilee and of Jesus being asleep in the bow of the ship. As he described the violence of the storm and the fear of the disciples, his eyes moved easily back and forth from the text to the crowd he was addressing. I looked over at Dad, and he was smiling and nodding his head.

As if on cue, Dad leaned over to me and whispered. "He knows the text, reads and speaks clearly, and is confident in his delivery. He is enthusiastic and holds the crowd's attention. Most importantly, it is clear that he expects people to listen to the Word and have the Word change them. If God is still raising up young men like this, there is more hope for our land than most people realize."

After an hour or more of young men preaching, our guy, Major, won the highest honors.

While everyone was heading for the fellowship hall for a reception and luncheon, we slipped out to the vehicle and headed out. We headed to the Cheddar's Scratch Made Kitchen for lunch. Trust me, if you are ever near one of those, it will be worth your time to go.

Dad and I got steaks (Dad says red meat is a good source of creatine, which helps to build muscle mass), and the girls got salmon or salads. We also enjoyed their chips and queso. And then, it was back to the room for a little study time. Not too long on that for me, though; Dad and I were meeting up with Parker Fellure at the gym mid-afternoon for a workout.

I was glad when that time finally came. Dad and I pulled up to the gym, met Parker there, and headed inside for what I like to call "clanking steel fellowship." Dad led us in a triceps workout, things like weighted dips, close-grip bench press, rope pulldowns, and a bunch more. That took about an hour, and then we did a subset of a different body group, which is something Dad always recommends. This time, we did a set of legs on the leg press. That turned out to be pretty cool; Brother Parker got a new personal best of 540 pounds!

We left the gym sweaty and happy. All guys, especially, should try to be as strong as possible; God made us to be warriors for those in need.

We prayed and parted ways, and Dad and I headed back to the hotel to begin the short (for us) and long (for the girls) process of getting ready for church. A couple of hours later, with everyone thoroughly poofed and primped, we headed back over to Victory Baptist Church. As expected, the service was really enjoyable. We always especially love the singing there. As Dad puts it, under Pastor Fellure, they do not just teach and preach theology; they even sing theology. And some of the songs they sang, as crazy as it sounds for people who are in church just about every single day, were songs that none of us had even heard before! But they were all so good; all of them sort of left me with the idea that God is high and holy while at the same time being present for His children at every single moment.

Once the singing was done, it was time for Dad to preach. He preached one of his newer messages, *Never Lose Your Identity*. It is a pretty cool message; he walks us all the way through the life of Daniel, from the time he was just a young kid being taken from his home all through his life until his final days. He shows all the drastic changes for Daniel along the way. Daniel actually spent a very tiny amount of his life in Jewish lands, wearing Jewish clothes, or speaking the Hebrew language. For nearly all of his life, he lived in Babylon or Persia, spoke the Babylonian language, was called by a Babylonian name, and dressed in Babylonian clothing. Yet, as an extremely old man, he was still so much the same person he started as that he was called "Daniel, of the captivity of the Children of Judah."

The point, of course, is that we should start our lives off early following God and never let any circumstances change that identity until the day we die.

There were a lot of people, but mostly young people, around the altar during the invitation. Dad prayed over all of them; Mom says he has a real heart for young people, and I believe it.

A little while later, we were in the Yukon, heading back to the hotel.

Tomorrow morning, we will go to a cool place nearby called Fort Pickens.

Tonight, we will go to Russia.

CHAPTER NINE

"Velcome bahck, cheeldren," The Conductor said as we woke.

"Ugghh," Aly grumped, "that cheesy faux-Russian accent sounds like something my dad would do."

"And I am sure he would do it well," the Conductor retorted with a laugh.

I could tell from the surroundings that God had answered our prayers and brought us right back to where we had stowed the Bibles. He's good like that.

"So, what is your plan on this day?" the Conductor inquired.

"Well, in general, we intend to find a way to cross the border with these Bibles, preferably without getting caught or killed, and get them to the underground church in Vyborg."

"I see," he said simply, though his words had kind of a "dad tone" to them that I recognized very well. Apparently, Carrie did, too.

"What is it?"

"Well, young lady, your brother's plan is more of a goal, really. A plan would need to include how exactly to do that. You see, just about every inch of that border is heavily guarded, both with human beings and with the barriers and technology of the day."

The girls both looked at me, and I could read the question on their faces.

"No, I don't exactly have a 'plan,' then," I said. "But we'll figure something out."

And then, something the Conductor said really hit me.

"Wait, what do you mean 'just about every inch?' Exactly what inches are there that are not heavily guarded?"

He wrinkled his brow, pursed his lips, and said, "I'm pretty sure you don't want to know that; it really isn't much of an option."

"Not MUCH of an option?" Carrie said inquisitively.

"Oh please, don't tell me you are getting more like Kyle on stuff like this!" he said with a grin.

"Maybe we are, maybe we aren't," she replied politely. "Either way, *an* option is better than *no* option, even if it is a *bad* option."

He nodded and was silent for a few seconds. I suspect he was thinking back to all of the other "not so advisable" things we had already done throughout our adventures. Finally, he spoke, and with reluctance.

"The Neva River is unguarded. It flows straight across the border from Finland into Russia and actually goes right past Vyborg. But please listen to me very carefully; there is a reason why it is unguarded. And the very specific reason it is unguarded is because the idea of running those rapids is absolutely insane, especially since the only crafts available to do so here in 1965 are rickety canoes."

"In other words," Aly said as she grinned from ear to ear, "fun for the whole family!"

The Conductor laughed and slowly shook his head from side to side. "So be it, then," he said with a touch of resignation. "If any kids are both capable enough to pull this off and walking closely enough with God to have Him aid them in the endeavor, I suspect it is you three."

We smiled and nodded and then, without a word, knelt together.

"Heavenly Father," I said with reverence, "here we are again, your kids, your Night Heroes. We have Bibles to be taken behind the Iron Curtain; a Sword that can pierce the devil's darkness. We also have a brave brother in Christ who is probably undergoing pretty severe torture right now and needs us to come to the rescue. Lord, for any of that to happen, we need some things. First off, we need you to help us find a canoe; we didn't exactly bring one with us. Secondly, we really need you to help us run these rapids safely. I know that as the oldest, I am responsible for bringing my brave little sisters home safely tonight. So please help all three of us to come through this safely together, to get the job done, and to get home to our folks. I pray all of this in Jesus' name, amen."

We stood to our feet, looked around, and as usual, the Conductor was gone. But I could not help but grin at what he had left behind.

"Check it out," I said as I smiled and pointed to a spot on the ground. The girls looked that way, and their eyes lit up. We were all very used to seeing the conductor's feet go six or seven steps and then just not be there anymore. But this time, while we were praying, he had made an unmistakable mark for us with his feet on the ground before he left for, um, "headquarters."

"A big arrow. Niiiiiiice," Carrie said as she nodded in approval. "I would say that can be safely followed."

Aly and I both obviously agreed, so we started off without another word. The sun was out and up that day, and the day was actually getting reasonably warm. And while this felt good to us as we walked, in the back of my mind, it was setting off alarm bells. Carrie, my genius sister, was obviously thinking exactly what I was thinking:

"This is going to make the rapids even worse, isn't it?"

"Yup, 'fraid so," I said matter-of-factly. "Snowmelt combined with the rapids of an already dangerous river is not a good combination. But, hey, if it were any other way, would it really be a normal life for us Night Heroes?"

She shrugged, and we all walked on in silence, save for the "Schlorp! Schlorp!" of our feet in the snow. I knew that, like me, my sisters were in their own thoughts right now. As for me, mine were on the rugged and raw beauty of this place. How in the world could anyone ever see such breathtaking beauty and not recognize that there had to be a Creator for it?

We walked on for an hour or so, and by now, we were paralleling the border. From somewhere way up ahead of us, I was beginning to hear the familiar and powerful sound of water.

"The Neva?" Carrie asked.

"I would say so. Let's keep our eyes open; we are looking for a canoe or something like it."

No sooner had the words come out of my mouth, we rounded a little bend and saw a tiny log cabin in a little clearing in the trees. Sure enough, right out front, there was a canoe tied to a tree.

"Welp, that's that!" Aly said cheerfully and started to bolt for the canoe. For the second time on this adventure, I snatched her up by the back of her jacket.

"Whoa, twerp, hold up. We can't exactly just go stealing private property for no good reason."

"No, you cannot," came the sound of a very aged female voice from behind us. We jumped and whirled around; I was not used to being caught flat-footed like that. When we landed, we found ourselves facing yet another deadly barrel, this time an old but clearly very well-cared-for shotgun. And, of all things, it was being held by an old lady who looked like she could have been every church's unofficial grandma to all the children.

"Hello, mummo," Carrie said sweetly, "and good day to you."

My jaw dropped, and I looked over at her, stunned.

"I googled a few important words when we were back home yesterday in case we might need them," she said with a shrug.

Mummo, grandma, in our language, lowered the gun just a bit.

"You are very polite and also very intelligent – for Americans, anyway," she said. We all ignored the thinly veiled insult; we knew that the Communists used the awesome power of propaganda to paint a picture of the West that was nowhere near correct.

"Thank you," Carrie said sweetly. "And now, since you are no doubt wondering why we are even here, please allow me to get right to the point since we are on a very tight schedule. We intend to smuggle Bibles into the Soviet Union, and we need to borrow your canoe to do so. Along the way, we intend to rescue a young man who has been imprisoned for doing the very same thing. So, may we borrow your canoe? I cannot guarantee that you will ever see it again."

I could feel all the breath leaving my body; I could not believe she was spilling all of the beans this openly and freely. This was either going to work like a dream or get us all killed; there would be no option in between.

For a second that seemed like an eternity, the gun stayed exactly where it was. Then, slowly, very slowly, the old lady dropped it to her side.

"I have no love for God – but I have nothing but pure hatred for the Soviets. They have taken everything from me, and now I live alone in these woods, mourning what once was."

Another moment of silence passed, and then the old woman whirled away from us and strode toward her cabin. "Take the canoe," she said over her shoulder, "I am too old to ever again use it anyway. And do not bother to tell me about your God, as I know you intend to do."

Two or three more steps, and the door slammed behind her. We were left alone in the yard, with the canoe – and three broken hearts. We stood there in stunned silence for a few seconds.

"I don't think I have ever seen anyone that bitter in my life," Aly said sadly.

"Me either, Squirt. I hate to think of all that she's lost along the way to make her like that."

Carrie was not talking. She had dropped her pack and was writing inside the front cover of one of the Bibles.

Dearest Mummo,

My name is Carrie, my sister is Aly, and my brother is Kyle. I am leaving you this Bible, and I ask you to read it, starting with the Gospel of Matthew. We do not know all you have been through or the depth of your loss. But we love you and I promise you that we will be praying for you from this day forward. Please receive Jesus as your Savior, and please meet us in Heaven one day. And though you will not understand this now, trust me when I tell you that it may be a very, very long time before we get there to join you.

Yours,
Carrie

БИБЛИЯ

I nodded with approval at everything Carrie had just written. We untied the canoe, and then I wrapped the Bible up in a bit of plastic to keep it safe and dry and left it near the old lady's front door for her to find later. Then we dragged the canoe down the hill and toward the sound of very angry, raging water.

CHAPTER TEN

As we stood on the banks of the river, I was very seriously rethinking the wisdom of this plan. Carrie stood beside me, and her words let me know she was thinking the exact same thing:

"People die in stuff like that, Kyle."

I nodded slowly. But I also knew that we had precisely zero other plans and no time to implement any other plans if we did have them.

I turned to the girls and laid out my thoughts.

"Okay, here's what we do. Carrie will be in front, Aly, you'll be in between us, and I will be in the rear."

"Why are you making her go up front?" Aly asked with annoyance in her voice. Carrie quickly answered her, though:

"Because canoes are steered from the back. His order makes sense; we will need his muscles to steer us through the rapids."

I nodded again. "No one is allowed to fall out; I repeat, no one is allowed to fall out. But if you do fall out, which you are not allowed to do, I need you to remember these words: 'nose up, toes up.'"

"Nose up/toes up?" Aly asked in utter confusion.

"Yes, Aly, nose up, toes up. If you fall out, roll over onto your back and keep your face up out of the water and keep your feet and toes out of the water as well, facing downstream. The main way that people die in rapids is by trying to stand up and then getting their feet caught under a rock as the water continues to push them forward. If you keep your nose up and toes up, that won't happen. Your patootie will get bruised up, but that is something you can live with."

"Got it. Nose up, toes up."

We put Aly into the middle of the boat, then put one pack of the Bibles at her feet in front of her, and then I got Carrie into the front of the boat. From there, I put the other two packs behind Aly and in front of where I would sit. That way, the bulk of the weight was in the back of the canoe, which would help to keep the front of it out of the water a bit.

"Here goes nothing, or everything," I said, and then I pushed the canoe into the water and jumped into the back.

Instantly, and I mean instantly, we were in a fight for our lives.

If you have never been on a raging river, you cannot possibly comprehend the absolute power of that water. Even in modern-day canoes, we would have struggled to navigate that hydrological Hades. "Whooooaaaaayyyyy!" I could hear Carrie screaming from the front above the din of the water, and I knew she was both scared to death and also losing her breath due to the cold of the water now soaking all of us to the bone. The canoe was pitching and dipping, and we were all instinctively shifting our weight to one side or the other, trying to keep it above water.

My muscles were screaming. I was fighting for everything I was worth to try to keep the boat facing forward; I knew that if it got sideways, we were all done for. Up front, Carrie was digging in with her paddle like a champion, greedily clawing at the water to try to help me keep it going in the right direction.

Aly was holding on for dear life; there was absolutely nothing she could do.

I looked up ahead, and my eyes got as wide as saucers. I could hear Carrie scream; we both knew we could not avoid the rock. We smashed into it – but thankfully, not quite head-on. Aly lurched to the side because of the impact and started to go airborne. I reached out and snagged her with my left hand and yanked her back into the boat with a thud.

"Kyle!" Carrie screamed again, and I could see her pointing up ahead as she did.

Of course; I mean, would it really be us if there wasn't a waterfall coming?

"Hooolllllddddddd onnnnnnnnn!" I screamed, and almost instantly, we could feel the river drop away from underneath us.

Thank God it was not a sheer drop; if it had been, we would all be dead. It was steep enough, though, that when we reached the bottom, the front of the canoe went straight down into the water, the back of the canoe rose up, and we were standing up on end! I could feel myself lurching forward as I desperately tried to hold both myself and Aly in the canoe. Instinctively, I leaned back and rolled my weight to the left, and the canoe began to turn, finally falling back onto its bottom, but with us now going backward!

"Carrie!"

"I know, I know!" she shouted back.

"Back on the right!" I barked, and she immediately began to paddle backward on the right side of the boat. At the same instant, I pulled forward with all of my might on the left side of the boat, and it began to turn. We finally got it completely righted, and then it was straight into another rapid. We steered between two rocks, perfectly executed a loop around a third, and I could feel us getting the hang of things.

We were in the rapids for probably ten more minutes, but they were getting less and less severe as we went, and we were getting more and more in command of things.

The rapids finally ended, and none too soon; I was absolutely, utterly, thoroughly spent.

Up ahead and to the left, we saw a sandy bank, and we made for it. I paddled as hard as I could with the energy that I no longer had, and we got it run ashore. Carrie crawled out and pulled the boat up a little further, then Aly followed her out the front and helped her to pull it up onto the bank even a bit more. I picked up the packs one at a time, tossed them ashore, took two steps, and fell out of the boat onto the shore on my back.

The girls sat down on either side of me. I looked up at them; they were ashen white and clearly as exhausted as I was.

"I think I figured out why the Conductor thought this was a bad idea," Carrie said dryly.

All I could do was laugh, an exhausted, hoarse, exhilarated laugh.

As much as we knew that the day was getting away from us, and as badly as we wanted to go ahead and get the Bibles to the underground church, I knew that we had a more pressing need for the next little bit. All of us were soaked to the bone, and the day was still cold enough in spite of the sunshine that we were all at risk of hypothermia.

I summoned the will to rise and started walking to some nearby trees. I took my pocket knife out and began to pry at some of the bark just over my head.

"What are you doing?" Aly asked.

"We need to get a fire started and get dried out and warmed up, Sis," I said, "and that means that we need some dry and fine material to work with. Dad taught me this when I was pretty young; 'the higher the dryer.' The stuff behind the bark, once you get several feet above ground level, will be dry enough to use as tinder. Carrie, take Aly and see if you can find some small twigs and also some stuff a little bit bigger than that."

A few minutes later, our collection pile was in a circle back in the trees and seemed to me to be plenty enough to work with. I made a ring out of rocks; this would help to bank the fire, and once the rocks warmed, they would radiate that heat for a while as well. I put the stuff I scraped from behind the bark, some people call it punk, into a little pile in the middle of my rock circle. Then I took a waterproof match from my pack – I have learned to carry things like that on these adventures – struck it and started the fire in that little pile. I blew on it softly, and it started to grow. Little by little, I added the tiny twigs the girls had brought. They ran for bigger things, and I continued to add to the pile as the fire grew. Within about ten minutes, we had a warm and respectable fire going.

We stayed around that fire for a couple of hours, turning like chickens on a spit, until we were finally completely dry and warm. Then, as everyone ought to do when they are leaving a fire in the wilderness, we put the fire completely out and doused it repeatedly with water.

And then we tossed the rocks aside and scattered every bit of it; we wanted to leave no trace that we had ever been there.

"Black Crow would be proud, I think," I said with a smile.[1]

The girls smiled back; great memories.

We hoisted and fastened our packs and started off downstream. By my reckoning, we should only be a few miles from Vyborg. I figured we could cover the distance to just outside the town today, but we would probably have to stow the Bibles and wait until tomorrow to get them to the church due to our delay around the fire.

For once, things actually worked out like I had planned.

---

[1] From The Night Heroes Vol. 4: The Blade of Black Crow

CHAPTER ELEVEN

The next morning, I was the one who was drooling on the pillow while the girls got up and about. And when I finally did wake up, every muscle in my body was aching; canoeing those rapids really did me in!

I finally managed to sit up on the side of the bed and then rise.

"Sore much, Grampa?" Carrie teased from the corner chair where she was sitting and reading her Bible.

"Yes, Carrie, yes I am," I said truthfully. "Where's Aly?"

"She and Mom and Dad are still down in the lobby having breakfast. I finished up first and came back up to read my Bible a bit more. I told Mom and Dad that you tossed and turned a lot last night; I didn't mention that you nearly drowned while doing so," she giggled.

I merely grunted, straightened my back, and shuffled to the bathroom. "*Is this the way adults feel all the time?*" I wondered. If so, growing up was definitely not for sissies.

I took a good bit more time than normal in the shower, letting the extremely hot water pound the soreness out of my muscles. Once I was dried off and dressed, I joined the rest of the family, including Carrie, down in the lobby. Dad was chomping at the bit to go; he was really excited to see Fort Pickens. Truthfully, all of us were; there is not much cooler than an old fort and all of the history that comes with it.

The fort most everyone goes to see in Florida is way down in Saint Augustine, the Castillo de San Marcos. And it is definitely worth seeing; it is in absolutely pristine condition after more than four hundred years. But from what Dad said, Fort Pickens is just as cool, only in other ways.

It took us about thirty minutes from the hotel to get down to the fort, and the day was beautiful all the way there, though maybe a little bit cloudier than yesterday. Maybe it was due to that extra little bit of cloud cover, but for whatever reason, there were not many people there; we just about had the place to ourselves.

Unlike the Castillo de San Marcos, at Fort Pickens, you do not have a tour guide. Fort Pickens is the biggest masonry fort in the entire state of Florida. So, with an enormous fort, very few people there, and no tour guide, we pretty much had the entire place to ourselves to explore at will.

We pretty quickly found that one of the coolest things about Fort Pickens is that there are a series of underground tunnels underneath it. Each one led to a dead end in the pitch-black darkness. As we soon discovered, they were self-destruct tunnels. Each one could hold 1027 pounds of gunpowder, gunpowder that was designed to blow the entire fort to smithereens if the walls were ever breached. Now that, friends, is some serious dedication to not giving the enemy what is yours! I kind of felt like there was a lesson in that. Not that any of us should ever destroy ourselves, obviously, but that we should be way more serious about not giving the devil so much as an inch of territory in our lives.

We explored that fort for a few awesome hours until we felt like we knew it well enough to have defended it ourselves if we had been there. And then I jerked as a thought hit me: one day, we very well might be!

"Hey," I whispered to Carrie as I slipped up beside her, "Pay close attention to all the details here. What if one day we end up getting sent back in time here on a mission?"

Her eyes got really wide, and Aly, who had overheard my whisper, let out a long "That would be coooooool!" under her breath.

This is an awesome life; I am glad God called us to it.

Maybe thirty feet up ahead of us, walking under an arched corridor, I saw Mom and Dad strolling, hand in hand. They had a pretty cool life, too; it was always really obvious how much they love each other and us.

When we were finally done exploring the fort, we all went back into Pensacola and found a cool place to eat called The Native Café. I had the fish tacos, and they were excellent. If you are ever in that area, I highly recommend it and them.

From there, we went back over to the Navarre Beach YMCA, and Dad and I got in a really good biceps workout. (OUCH!) Then it was back to the hotel. We hastily got cleaned up and ready for church and headed down the stairs to get to the parking lot and the Yukon. When we have the option, we always take the stairs instead of the elevator; Dad has taught us to do simple things like that that add a little bit of cardio to our day. I grinned as I thought of that; if he knew how much cardio the girls and I had gotten last night, he may have let us take the elevator instead!

After our standard twenty-minute ride, we were pulling into the parking lot of the Victory Baptist Church again. Tonight and tomorrow night would be extra special; Dad would not be the only preacher. Along with him, Brother Joe Arthur would be preaching, and he is one of our absolute favorites. Dad always likes to tell preachers, "Brother Joe won't hurt you." And I know why he says that. For some reason, every now and again, you will find a preacher who seems intent on ripping a pastor's flock to shreds as he preaches. But Brother Joe, while faithfully preaching the Word, is encouraging, funny, and lively. And he is nice to little people; he is as likely to be found sitting down talking to a bunch of kids as to a bunch of important preachers.

The music in the service was wonderful, as always. Have you ever heard "The Cleansing Wave"? It's an old song, but man, it is a good one!

Dad was the first preacher tonight. He preached a nearly brand-new message, *No Bones In Ziklag*. It comes from 1 Samuel 30 and is all about the time that David made a terrible mistake by going to Philistine territory to escape Saul. While he was there, he and his men got drafted into the army. And then, of all things, they were called up to go fight against their own people, Israel! Fortunately, some of the lords of the Philistines saw them and recognized them and refused to let them come to battle with them, fearing that they may turn on them during the fight.

David and his men had to be breathing a sigh of relief and laughing on their way back to Ziklag, the city that they had been given to live in. But then, they saw smoke rising from the city; while they were away, the Amalekites had attacked and burned everything to the ground. Obviously, every man there would have been terrified that their wives and children had been murdered. But as they went through the charred wreckage of the city, there was something missing; there were no bones in Ziklag. That let them know that everyone was still alive and out there somewhere. So they consulted God using a special thing called the Ephod, which I don't quite understand, and asked if they should pursue after everyone and if they would recover everyone. God told him to do so and that they would.

And they did.

But the reason they even knew to try, the reason they knew there was hope, is because there were no bones in Ziklag. Dad used that to point out that as long as the people we are concerned for are still alive, there is always hope. That encouraged me; there are some people that I really love who are lost, and I have been praying for a very long time that they will get saved.

Once that was done, and after a few more songs, the pastor got up to introduce Brother Joe. But before he did, he dropped a bomb on three kids in that service – me and Carrie and Aly. Mind you, he didn't understand that that's what he did, but we understood it.

"Before Brother Joe comes to preach, I have an important announcement to make. The meeting is obviously supposed to last through tomorrow night. But as all of you have obviously noticed, we have had a great number of people out sick this week. And tonight, many more called in earlier to say that they are now sick as well. So, for everyone's safety and benefit, tonight will be the last night of the meeting. So let's make it a good one; everyone listen carefully and respond to the message. Brother Joe, come preach to us."

My jaw was hanging open, and my eyes were wide. I looked over my sisters, and they both looked at me with the exact same look on their faces.

This was a disaster. I knew Dad well enough to know that because the meeting was ending tonight, in the morning, we would be packed up and heading down the road to get to our next planned destination a day early. We had planned on having two days to get everything done in the U.S.S.R., and now we would have to get it done tonight, or it would not get done at all.

We knew that Pastor Fellure had made the exact right call; every pastor ought to carefully take care of his people. And Brother Joe did a fantastic job, as always. People hung on his every word for nearly an hour, and everyone got some encouragement and help from the Lord.

Since it was, unexpectedly, our last night, a bunch of us ended up at the Whataburger for some extra food and fellowship after the service. We sat around a big table with Brother Joe and the pastor and his family and mostly just listened to all of them tell stories about the ministry. Let me tell you, funny stuff happens in the church world! And especially when you have great storytellers like Brother Joe and Pastor Fellure and my dad, we were absolutely in stitches for hours.

Finally, though, everyone had to part ways for the night and for the next little while. We knew there was a chance we may see each other again at Brother Ricky Gravley's meeting in Rossville, Georgia, in a few months, if everyone's schedule worked out for that.

After praying with each other, we all headed to our different vehicles and back to our various hotels or houses, as the case may be.

As for us Night Heroes, the tension was building; we had exactly one more night to bust Sergei out of KGB headquarters and get him to safety across the border.

And if we failed, we would either be dead or locked behind the Iron Curtain forever.

CHAPTER TWELVE

We woke up right where we had left the Bibles the night before, back in the trees, easy walking distance from Vyborg. It was still dark, and I could see the Conductor poking at a low fire he had kindled a few feet away from us.

Carrie and Aly woke up at about the same time, yawned, stretched, and the three of us joined the Conductor at the fire.

"So," he began simply, "your timetable has been shortened."

"Yes, sir, it appears so. But we will give every ounce of our energy and abilities to getting the job done today, I assure you."

"I know you will. Above all, the Father knows you will; that kind of thing is exactly why you were chosen to begin with."

There were three little metal cups of coffee steaming by the fire. We nodded our thanks and picked them up to drink. Later, when we talked about that moment, we found out that each cup tasted exactly like our favorite kind; mine had a French vanilla flavor to it, Carrie's was mocha, and Aly's was peppermint.

Our Father really does think of everything.

Presently, I could just barely see the edge of that part of the world turning from black to pink as the sun made its way toward daybreak. The girls and I finished off our coffee, we and the Conductor put the fire out, and then we shook his hand and thanked him for all he had done for us. He merely nodded, and the three of us Night Heroes knelt down to pray.

"Heavenly Father," I pleaded, "we have many miles to go on this day, and we do not know all of the dangers that we will face along the way. Our time is shorter than we had anticipated, and there is a lot riding on everything we do and every decision we make. Please, Father, help us to be what we cannot be on our own; help us to be enough. We pray all of this in Jesus' name, amen."

We rose to our feet and did not even look around for the Conductor. We knew he was gone, and we knew we had to hurry.

It only took us a few moments to get the packs loaded up on our backs. Fortunately, in this time and in this place, it was not at all uncommon to see people walking around with fairly sizable packs. And since everyone would assume that if we had crossed the border, our packs had been checked, we were not likely to encounter any problems on the first part of our mission on this day.

The pastor had given us very good instructions and a very good description of how to find the underground church in Vyborg. This one would not be out in the sticks like the one across the border in Finland; it would be right in town, in the back room of a bakery.

As we entered the town, it almost felt like stepping back into an old movie. The streets were all cobblestone, but a dirty and broken kind of cobblestone through years of neglect. They could have been very pretty if they had been maintained. Most of the buildings seemed to be a type of hand-mixed masonry: solid but not very artistic. Everything seemed, well, gray, for lack of a better word. There were very few splashes of color anywhere save for a few pots of what seemed to be pansies struggling for their existence.

As we passed down the street, no one made eye contact. Young or old, everyone seemed to be preoccupied with staying out of trouble, mostly by not interacting with anyone. Man, life under Communism was every bit the misery my dad always described it as from his studies of history. His grandfather had actually taught history for many years at a University, majoring on the Cold War era and the horrors of Communism.

As we rounded a street that we were looking for, a street marked by an old church with a broken church bell, we knew by our noses that we were going in the right direction.

"That's fresh bread!" Aly said with excitement.

"Yes, it is!" I answered back with excitement equaling hers.

Following our noses, we soon came to the bakery that I knew had a very precious secret in the back of it. We walked in and walked up to the counter. In seconds, a tall, thin man with a pointy white beard approached us from behind the counter."

"Chto by vy khoteli?" he asked pleasantly.

I started to answer in English, but Carrie beat me to it – in Russian, of all things!

"Manna, pozhaluysta."

The man looked at her, clearly surprised – but nowhere near as surprised as I was.

She turned to me a bit, smiled, and said, "Remember that Russian grammar book I was reading on our trip to Oklahoma?"[2]

I just nodded, with my mouth still hanging open.

"There you go," she said simply.

"You are American," Gandalf (I had already decided to call him that until I knew his name) replied.

"Yes, sir, we are," I said. "And my sister is correct. We came here with Manna."

The man smiled but also looked warily past us into the street. After seeing that we had not been followed, he moved to the door, put up a sign that I am guessing meant something like "We will be

---

[2] From The Night Heroes Vol. 12: Deadline

back in fifteen minutes," motioned to us with his hand, and simply said, "Follow me."

Gandalf made his way out of the tiny front room, down a very thin hall, and stopped at the back wall. There was a bare light bulb in a fixture at the upper right corner of that wall, with a pull cord hanging down from it. He reached up to the pull cord, flicked it on and off three times, and then stood there patiently for a few seconds.

We heard a slow creaking, and then, much to my surprise, the back wall began to shift aside – it was a fake, a doorway completely disguised as the back wall of the hallway.

I took a moment to let that sink in; these people were having to be incredibly creative and ingenious just to find a way to meet for worship – right down to having to install secret doors that led to secret rooms. That kind of puts most of our excuses to skip church as Americans to shame.

As we made our way into that hidden back room, I could see, just as I suspected, a light bulb right on the other side of that door. The flicking of the light three times on our side also flicked it on and off three times on the hidden side, letting them know that it was safe to open.

Inside the room, as my eyes adjusted to the semi-darkness, I saw about a dozen people gathered around a piece of paper on the table. They were so intent on it that most of them had not even noticed we had entered the room.

"Excuse me, sir, what letter are they reading?" Aly asked in utter innocence.

"Not a letter, child; one page of a letter. That is a single leaf of the book of Philippians."

For what seemed to be the hundredth time on this mission, all three of us Warner kids had our jaws drop open at the exact same moment.

"A page. They are all reading and completely absorbed by one single page of the book of Philippians?"

"Yes, young man. Bibles are very hard to come by in this part of the world; when we get them, we often split them up into pieces and circulate them to those who desire to know the Book. We had been anticipating a small delivery of them to come to us recently, but they did not arrive; our courier was taken, and the Bibles he was bearing were taken with him."

"Yes, sir, we know. Sergei. He is why we are here. We have replacements for the Bibles that were taken."

Everyone in the room gasped at the word Bible; they all knew that word. We three set our packs down, opened them up, opened up the plastic bags that were within them, and began setting the Bibles out in stacks on the table.

Every single person in the room who was not a Night Hero began to cry. They made their way to those stacks, picked up Bibles individually, held them to their chests, and sobbed.

And now we were crying along with them.

I made up my mind then and there to never take my Bible for granted again.

Everyone in the room found their own place to sit down and started reading one of those Bibles.

"They will each have them read from cover to cover within the next seventy-two hours," Pastor Gandalf said simply. "Thank you. Thank you for bringing a light into the darkness at great personal risk to yourselves. This is the Sword that will eventually bring down the empire of evil and the Iron Curtain that surrounds it, granting liberty to the captives.

"I am Pastor Alexandre," he said. "You need not tell me your names; in this area of the world, the less one knows, the better."

I was a little bit disappointed, actually. Not that he did not want to know our names, but that I could not think of him as Pastor Gandalf anymore.

"Pastor," I said, "we are glad to have brought you the Sword. But that is not the only thing that we are here to do. We promised the church in Finland, which is worried about Sergei, that we would get him free and get him home. So, what we need to know from you is, where is the local KGB headquarters, and how hard would it be for us to break into it?"

His eyes got wide – and then he laughed a deep, genuine, but somehow frightening laugh.

"It is merely six blocks from here; we operate under the very shadow of the enemy. And it will not be hard at all to break into. No one in their right mind ever tries to get into KGB headquarters; everyone wants to avoid it. Getting in will be easy; getting out, not so much. Getting out of town and out of the country, if you do get out of KGB headquarters, impossible. Save for God, of course; anything is possible with Him.

I nodded in agreement. And then I threw up a figurative Hail Mary:

"A car. Could we possibly get a car somehow?"

The pastor smiled. "Certainly; you are welcome to steal mine."

"Steal?" I said with confusion.

"Yes, steal," he replied firmly. "If I give it to you, I will be arrested and sent to the gulag forever. If you steal it, I am merely the latest in a long line of crime victims in this hopeless land, and no one will think a thing of it. So, here," he said as he handed me his keys, "steal my car. It is the brown, four-door Moskvitch 408 on the corner. The carburetor sticks a little, so the ride can be a bit jerky.

"Leave it as far away from here as possible; I do not need any suspicion to land on my flock."

I shook the thin man's hand, thanked him, and then I asked him to pray over me and my sisters. Any man faithfully pastoring in such conditions was a man I figured I could trust to get a prayer through.

"Dear God of glory," he began in the most reverent of voices, "I do not know these, my young brother and sisters in the Lord. I do know that they have risked everything to bring your Word to where it is most needed. And I know that they further intend to risk their own lives and safety to try and free another. Children like this are rare; as always, You have raised up warriors from the least expected places.

"Go, then, with these thine soldiers. Grant them wisdom beyond their years and strength beyond their means. Grant them victory over any device of the evil one. Provide for them the light when there is no light and allies from among their seeming enemies.

"These things I implore in the name of the matchless Christ, amen."

We three shook the old man's hand one by one; he did not seem like the hugging type.

"Steal the car, use it to scout the town and see which way you intend to make your escape, and then may God help you as you do the unthinkable. I will not report the car stolen until closing time when I would normally have noticed it gone; that should give you time to do what you need to do."

We thanked the dear man again and then went out to "steal" his car.

"Easiest carjacking in history," Carrie quipped.

"I would say so," I said as we opened the doors and sat down in the seats. "Except for the fact that this thing is an absolute antique and rattletrap. Let's hope everything works."

I stuck the key in the ignition, pumped the gas pedal a couple of times, and turned the key. It sounded like what I imagine death might sound like if you were trying to wake him up and get him out of bed, but fortunately, it actually started. I was glad for the instruction to drive it around a bit, not just so that we could scout the area but so that I could familiarize myself with the car in case we needed to do any fancy driving to try and escape.

We drove all around the town several times, and then I finally pulled over on a back road to gather my thoughts before we headed to KGB headquarters.

And that is where, as my dad would put it, "the wheels came off of the day."

CHAPTER THIRTEEN

"Kyle! Kyle! Look!" Aly shouted from the back seat.

I looked at where she was pointing out the side window of the backseat, and my heart sank while my stomach jumped up into my chest. This was not good. A girl, maybe early twenties, was being attacked by three full-grown men who were clearly intent on robbing her or maybe worse.

I reached for the door handle, and Carrie grabbed my arm.

"Kyle, if you get involved, not only may Sergei never make it home, WE may never make it home."

"So, are you saying we shouldn't get involved?" I asked incredulously.

"Nope. We should. Just wanted to make sure you understand the ramifications going into it."

"He understands," Aly shouted angrily, "now let's go pound the snot out of them!"

Three doors flung open, and in mere seconds, we were on them. I smashed into one jerk with my shoulder at full speed, catching him shoulder-high from his side and sending him sprawling across the ground like he had been hit by a truck. Carrie and Aly both dove full speed into the legs of another, sending him sprawling as well. Then they were all over him, smashing, scratching, biting, and generally making the guy feel like two Tasmanian devils had made it their mission to destroy his life. The third disengaged from the girl and started to reach for Carrie and Aly to yank them off. Unfortunately for him, I got to him first, grabbing him in a bear hug from behind and slamming him to the ground. Then I piled on top of him and began to unleash punch after punch into his face with all my power.

I hit him seven or eight times and would have hit him again, except that the first guy I knocked down had now gotten up and was rushing toward me. I pushed myself up halfway and unleashed a sidekick into him as he charged me. I caught him right in the gut, knocking every bit of the wind out of him. Then, in fury, I did something I had never tried before: I grabbed him by the back of his belt and the back of his collar, picked him up over my head like I was doing a military press, and brought him slamming into the ground, putting him out cold.

Carrie and Aly had set their guy running for his life and got to me right as I did my power slam on him.

"Duuuuuuude! That was EPIC!" Aly squealed with delight. Carrie, though, ever watchful, brushed past me and went to the young lady, who was sobbing on the ground.

"Tee v bee za pasnosti," she said as she reached down to her with both hands.

Instantly, the young lady stopped crying. "American?" she asked.

"Yes," Carrie said, "how did you know?"

"Your Russian for 'you are safe' is good, but your accent is terrible," she replied, and all three of us lost it laughing. That seemed to lighten the mood of the young lady as well, who then laughed a bit herself and took Carrie by both hands as Carrie helped her to stand.

"I did not mean to insult you," she said apologetically, "You saved me; that is another way I knew you were not from here. None of our people will take the risk of getting involved to help others."

"We are honored to have been able to do so," I said with the warmest smile I could muster. "It is what our Heavenly Father would have us do."

Instantly, I stopped, stunned at what I had just said and the trouble I had possibly caused us by saying it publicly, and to someone we did not know.

"Good grief, Bro," Carrie hissed, "careless, much?"

"Christians?" the young lady said in shock.

Oh boy. What now? I never actually dreamed we would come to a moment where we must either deny Christ for our own safety or admit that we were believers and possibly lose our lives. Is this how the early Christians felt every single day?

But I knew there really was no option, not for us Warners. Not for any true believer, really.

"Yes, we are," I said firmly. And then I stood there beside my sisters, waiting for whatever horrible thing would happen next. Whatever it was, we would face it together.

"I am Katarina," she said. And then she put her hand to her neck, grasped a necklace that was hanging down inside her shirt, and pulled it out. She held it up for us to see – and I smiled what was probably the most relieved smile of anybody in human history. There, in her hand, at the end of that chain, was a cross.

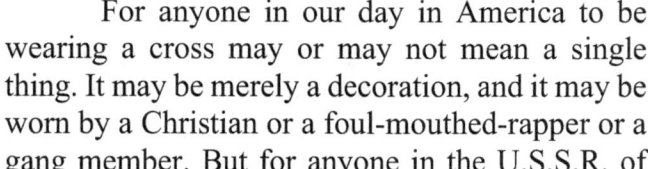

For anyone in our day in America to be wearing a cross may or may not mean a single thing. It may be merely a decoration, and it may be worn by a Christian or a foul-mouthed-rapper or a gang member. But for anyone in the U.S.S.R. of 1965 to be wearing a cross, even one kept unseen under a shirt, really did mean something.

"My mother gave it to me the day I received Christ as my Savior as a nine-year-old little girl," she said with a tearful smile. My father, he has never understood, so we do not speak of it. And oftentimes, my faith has wavered. I have wondered so often where is God in all of this hopelessness. And yet, today, as I was being attacked, I prayed – I admit shamefully that I have not done so for weeks; my faith has been on the verge of ruin. And yet, God heard and answered my prayer anyway, bless His holy name."

And then she did something I would never have expected. She unclasped the chain, slipped around Carrie's neck, and clasped it before Carrie could even react.

"Do not forget me," she said. "And never doubt God, for I pray that I will never doubt Him again. And tell everyone in the West what believers are facing here behind the Iron Curtain. Tell everyone to pray that one day we will be free to worship God in the light, not just in the shadows."

And then she turned and ran.

We did, too, back to the car. We were getting later by the minute. If there were many more interruptions, we were not going to get this job done.

CHAPTER FOURTEEN

We drove around the block a couple of times for us to catch our breath from the fight. But knowing how tight the timing was getting, we pretty quickly drove right to KGB headquarters and parked across the street.

"Do I even need to ask if we have a plan for this one?" Carrie said dryly.

"Nope," I said. "We go in, we figure it out on the fly, we grab our guy, and we get gone like tax dollars in Washington."

Carrie just rolled her eyes and then rolled with the plan/not a plan.

We exited the car, walked calmly across the street, and straight into the unmarked doors of KGB headquarters for Vyborg. We walked straight through the lobby, and the lady behind the desk never once even looked up at us. Opening the door straight in front of us, we walked through it and made our way down the hallway. There were closed doors on each side and a stairway branching off both to the right and to the left at the end of that hallway.

I motioned with my hand to the right, and both of the girls took that staircase while I took the left. I hoped, but was by no means certain, that they joined in the basement. I was going for the basement because, as near as I could figure from old movies that may or may not be accurate, that is where all the "we have ways to make you talk" would be taking place.

I came out at the bottom on my side and walked through a door in the corner of a room at the exact same moment that the girls walked through the door in the other corner of the room. I quickly surveyed the room and took in all that was happening, and I knew my sisters were doing the same.

There was one disheveled and badly beaten man tied to a chair; that would be Sergei.

There was a group of six weaselly-looking KGB agents around him, all wearing the thick rubber gloves they had been taking turns beating him with; those would be our next victims.

Immediately, Aly whipped out her ever-present slingshot and went to town. At her request, Dad had upgraded her to mid-sized metal balls to shoot with, thinking she was merely shooting at targets in our time. Boy, was that unfortunate for the people we were about to wreck.

In mere seconds, she had thwacked two KGB dudes in their big foreheads, sending them screaming and writhing to the ground. I had closed the gap to the others, vaulted across a table, and kicked one of them in the chest, sending him crashing into the wall and out of commission.

Carrie was a bit more sedate; she calmly walked up to two others who reached out to grab her just as she whipped out the mace and sprayed them both in the face. They joined Aly's two victims screaming on the ground.

The last man standing had reached for his gun – and managed to get it out before I could reach him.

That did not end so well for him; a well-placed shot from my deadly little sister shattered his hand and sent the gun skittering across the floor. He bent over in agony, holding his hand and screaming, and I ended his noise with an uppercut to his face that substantially rearranged everything on it.

"Fun times," I said, and then quickly pulled out my pocket knife and cut Sergei loose.

"Can you stand? Can you walk?"

"Yes, and yes," he said weakly. "Anything to get out of here."

Carrie and I got on either side of him and helped him stand. He wobbled a bit and then started taking some slow steps forward.

"I hate to rush you after all you have been through," I said, "but we really do need to hurry as much as you are able."

He lurched forward a little faster, and we got him to the stairs that I had come down just a moment earlier. It took all three of us to help him get to the top of them; the poor guy was in really bad shape and badly winded.

We gave him a second to catch his breath, and then we calmly walked down the hallway toward that same door that would lead us into the lobby. I was not worried about anyone up here hearing anything from down there; I knew it would be (intentionally) mostly soundproof because of the activities they engaged in.

We got to the door, opened it, and casually walked through the lobby once again. I cut my eyes over to the receptionist, and once again, she never even looked our way. I would have chalked that up to God keeping her occupied, but I suspected that it was also mostly that no one in this part of the world had any incentive to do a good job at anything.

I was relieved when we made it out the door and started down the steps to cross the street to our waiting vehicle. We got to the car, got Sergei settled in the back with Carrie, and Aly got up front with me. As calmly as I could, I eased the car out into traffic and started heading down the street, out of town, and toward the border.

CHAPTER FIFTEEN

Once we got out of town, I opened that old rattletrap up as fast as it would go. We only had twenty-four miles to get to the border, but I wanted to put some distance between us and the scene we had just made back in KGB headquarters.

"So, and please tell me you have one," Carrie said, "what is the plan to get across the border once we get there?"

All three pairs of eyes stared at me. I was used to two; it felt kind of weird to have another pair of eyes joining them, especially a pair of eyes that were black and swollen from the beating they had been taking.

I dodged the question for a moment so I could think. "Sergei, did they get anything out of you? Is the church at risk?"

Out of the corner of my eye, I could see him smile weakly.

"No. They got nothing. But if it had gone on much longer, they would have gotten everything; they had sent for the dentist."

The confused look on my face told him that I did not know what he meant, so he quickly explained. "The dentist, as they call him, pulls healthy teeth one by one with no anesthetic until a man is willing to talk."

Ouch. No wonder everybody hated the KGB.

"So, to your sister's question, you have sprung me from the clutches of the KGB, but do you have any plan to get across the border? If not, we will all be toothless soon, if not dead."

"Only a vague one," I said truthfully. "I read about it once. There are guards with guns at the border, but the engine of a car will usually catch most of the bullets. I intend to put you lying down in the backseat and my sisters in the trunk and pile tree branches all around you for extra protection from bullets coming from the side and above, and simply charge the border, laying as far back in the seat as I can hoping for the engine to protect me from the bullets coming from straight ahead."

He let out a low whistle and said, "That really is a terrible plan."

"SEE?!?" Carrie and Aly both shouted at the exact same time, "It's not just us!"

"I feel like I say this a lot, but do you, do ANY of you have a better plan at this moment?"

All three of them went totally silent. And then Sergei spoke again.

"Do you always travel by the bottom of your breeches?"

That one took me a minute – then I started to laugh when I finally got it.

"Fly by the seat of our pants, you mean. And, yes, in fact, we do."

"That's the way we roll, baby!" Aly said cheerfully.

Without even looking, I knew that Carrie had her eyes shut tightly and was shaking her head back and forth as if in disbelief.

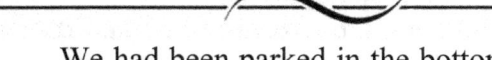

We had been parked in the bottom part of a field by the tree line for nearly an hour; it had taken me that long to pack Sergei and my sisters in like sardines amidst all of the branches I had broken and piled around them. I was soaked to the bone in sweat, which is a pretty horrible thing in the cold weather.

"Okay, everybody," I said as firmly as I could in my breathless condition, "sit tight and be quiet. Oh, and I recommend you pray as well; once I start this car, I do not intend to stop until we get through the border."

I could hear Sergei mumbling something in his native tongue, and I suspected it was not encouraging.

"What he said," Carrie replied from under foliage, confirming my guess.

Undaunted, I opened the door and sat down in the driver seat, prayed a quick and desperate prayer, and drove back up onto the road and for the border. We had about seven more miles to go; I had stopped far enough back, I hoped, not to be noticed while we prepared.

I was driving pretty slow, maybe forty miles per hour. I did not want to appear nervous or panicked as we made our way to the border and a bunch of jumpy, angry, and heavily armed border guards.

"I see it up ahead," I hissed. I was not sure if any of my passengers/packages could hear me underneath all of their padding.

There were five cars in line ahead of me, all of them about as decrepit as the one that I was driving. I watched intently to see how the process would go with each one.

"Three guards per car," I murmured. "One comes to the driver's door to demand to see his papers. The other goes to the passenger door and stands beside it with a gun at the ready. The third literally stands in front of the vehicle with his gun pointed at the hood. Yikes."

Once the guard at the driver's door was satisfied with whatever paperwork he had checked, paperwork that we definitely did not have, he nodded to the others, they moved off to the side, and then he waved the vehicle forward. It proceeded slowly ahead, then stopped on the other side as the driver spoke to yet another set of guards. On each side of that section of road, there was a three-story guard tower with machine guns on tripods pointing down the road, ready for a guard to use them if necessary.

The second car had now cleared the paperwork guard and was moving forward. The procedure was the exact same way as the first and pretty much the same snail's pace.

"Two down, three to go," I whispered under my breath.

A few moments later, the third car cleared the paperwork guard and started moving forward.

"Three down, two to –"

And that is as far as I got.

Somehow, the icy cold barrel of a gun unexpectedly pushing into my cheek made me not want to finish the sentence.

CHAPTER SIXTEEN

"Take your hands off of the steering wheel and put them in your lap very slowly," came the crisp, clear English in a Russian accent.

"Yes sir, doing so now, sir," I said as I slowly lowered my hands to my lap, palms down.

"I am going to take a step back. You are going to exit the car, slowly. My gun will be trained on you the entire way."

It was not a request, nor was I inclined to treat it as one.

I very slowly and smoothly opened the car door, raised both of my hands where they could be seen, stepped out of the car, and stood up straight. I found myself looking at the young soldier with the gun, an equally young soldier with a gun just to the left of him, and a few feet further back to my left, an older and clearly high-ranking military official who looked as serious as a blood clot.

"Is there no firewood in America? Surely, there must be some reason you have come all the way to the U.S.S.R. to collect ours. Let me guess;

you have people underneath these branches, and you hoped the branches would shield them from bullets as you rush the border."

With no other valid option, I copped to the accusation.

"Yes, sir, that is, in fact, exactly what I intended. I have a gentleman in the backseat, and my sisters are in the trunk.

"Your plan is absolutely terrible," he said bluntly.

"SEE?!?" I heard from both the trunk and the back seat. Man, this was getting embarrassing.

"Dig them all out," the man said to his underlings as he wheeled to walk away, "and bring them straight to me."

It took a few minutes, but the soldiers finally got Carrie and Aly and Sergei unpacked; I had really wedged them all in tightly. Once that was done, he pointed out a line of low buildings off to the right of the border crossing and said, "March,"

"How do we know which one to march to?" I said, since both of the guards were behind us.

"Don't worry," he said pleasantly. "If you start to go the wrong direction, we will shoot you, and you will know."

"Well, now, that's encouraging," Carrie quipped.

Since the man in charge seemed to be a pretty important individual, I evaluated the buildings as we walked toward them and saw that one of them had two guards standing at either end of the porch. I knew without asking that that was where we were going, so I went that direction.

"Good guess, American," he said, "maybe not all of you are not quite so dumb as we have heard."

I was grateful that, for once, Carrie chose not to wield that acidic tongue of hers with some clever retort; I was still kind of hoping to live to get out of all this.

"Halt," the two guards on the porch said as they stood and converged shoulder to shoulder at the top of the steps.

"We will take it from here," they said to the guards that marched us there.

Those guards saluted, then whirled and walked away. The two guards at the top of the porch separated, one opened the door, and the voice from inside simply said, "Enter – all of you."

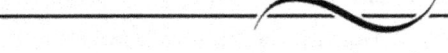

A moment later, the four of us were standing in front of a large metal desk that reminded me of something a high school principal might have used a long time ago. The room was sparse, with just the barest of furnishings. The man behind the desk, though, was still terrifying.

"Americans, all alike," he said with dripping contempt. "You feel like you can come and go at will, and there will be no consequences. All of this I know; what I do not know, but will know soon because you are going to tell me, is why three Americans and one Finnish dog are in my land and trying to get out of my land."

"As for you," he said as he angled his face to look at Sergei, "from the looks of you, you have already had some dealings with the KGB. So, criminal, we shall start with you. Why are you here, what have you done, and why are you walking free?"

Sergei stood stone-faced, saying nothing.

The man smiled, calmly picked up a pistol, aimed it at Sergei, and pulled the trigger. I jumped as the noise of the shot rang through the small building. The girls screamed. I looked down, and Sergei was writhing on the floor, with blood coming from his upper arm.

"Who wants to be next?" He screamed.

"Me. I do." I said as I stepped in front of Carrie and Aly.

The man came out from behind the desk. The two big guards had not moved from the corners of the room behind us. He got right in front of me and put the barrel of the gun against my forehead.

"Go get me four body bags and a truck," he said to the two guards. Immediately, they left the room to retrieve some things that we really did not want them coming back with.

"They are good men," he said, "utterly loyal to me. They will do whatever I say. Now, before I pull the trigger four times, one for you and one for each of them, and one to finish off your friend that I merely nicked with my first shot, I have exactly one question... for you," he said as he looked over at Carrie.

My eyes grew wide, but I dared not move. If he went for either of my sisters...

"Do you or do you not have a cross around your neck?"

It felt like time stood still.

"Yes sir, I do," she said as she unfastened the chain, pulled it out, and handed it to him. The right hand that held the gun to my forehead never wavered. With his left hand, though, he opened his palm to receive the cross and chain from Carrie. Then he held up the chain to let the cross dangle a bit in the air.

Yep, we were all definitely dead.

"Katarina..." he said with a slight shake of the head and what looked like maybe possibly a tiny little smile.

I lost my breath. I looked square in the man's face, taking note of his cheekbones, his nose, his chin.

"Your daughter," I said.

"Yes, my daughter," he said. "When she called me earlier to tell me that she had been attacked and had been rescued by a brave American young man and his two equally brave sisters, at first, I did not believe her. But then I realized that she has always told the truth – even about things that I did not want to hear. Imagine my surprise, then, when watchers told me they had spied Americans driving toward the border in a stolen car. Normally, I would leave such a thing to my men and simply have them capture you and turn you over to the KGB. But I had to know if it was you. Above all, I had to know if this God my daughter believes in had actually gotten so specific as to have you rescue her and then come to me.

"You must admit, such a coupling of events is the most unlikely of coincidences," he said.

"You are correct, sir," I said with a bit of relief, though I knew we were not out of the woods yet. "There are no coincidences with God. In fact, our being here is way more miraculous than you might imagine, though we are not at liberty to discuss those details with you. It is clear, though, that through your daughter and through us, God is trying to send you a message."

"Let me guess," he said with a wry smile, "I must repent of my sins and receive Jesus Christ as my Lord and Savior."

"It sounds like your daughter has been witnessing to you," Aly said. "You should listen to her."

"Should I? I just might, little one, I just might. Would it make you happy if I promised to speak to her of this tonight?"

"It would make me very happy," Aly said with a million-watt smile.

"Then consider it done," he said firmly.

This was a really cool moment, I knew that. But I also was still sort of concerned about that "not out of the woods" thing.

"Um, sir, does this mean that we will not be needing those four body bags? I mean, we really don't want to need those body bags."

His face grew stone serious.

"Oh, we will definitely be needing the body bags," he said. "After all, I am a loyal Soviet."

And then he pulled the trigger four times.

CHAPTER SEVENTEEN

When my ears stopped ringing and my eyes finally peeked open, I realized that no one was dead. I mean, no one other than the plant by the door; it was now lying in the wreckage of dirt and a shattered pot.

I looked at Katerina's father in bewilderment.

"You can't exactly walk out of here and past the guards, now can you? But do you know what you can do? You can ride out in body bags in the back of a truck once I tell the guards that my men are going to dump some dead bodies out on the other side of the border to send a message to the Finns."

Then he turned to Carrie and extended the cross and chain out to her.

"I believe this is yours, a gift from my daughter," he said with love in his voice.

Carrie extended both of her hands, put the cross and chain into his, and closed his hand around it.

"Give it back to your daughter, please. Tell her we said thank you. Let her know that her gift saved our lives. Tell her that every time she looks at it, she should remember to never let her faith grow weak; God knows exactly where she is and has never forgotten her for even a moment."

The man smiled and nodded, putting the cross and chain in his pocket.

A few moments later, four dead bodies/not dead bodies passed through the Iron Curtain and into freedom on the other side.

Coming Soon:
Escape From Beaver Island

America has never had a king – or has she? Apparently, there was indeed a king, at least on Beaver Island. But this king was neither noble nor nobility. This king was a common thief with enough charisma to turn his own highjacked cult into a monarchy. And he and his followers did a great job of "appropriating supplies from the nearby Gentiles" to keep their little kingdom running well.

They did an equally great job of keeping people in the fold, even when they no longer wanted to be there and even when they were going to have to marry into the creepy king's harem.

As it turns out, God has a solution for that kind of thing.

A three-member, rough-and-tumble, always looking for a fight solution called the Night Heroes.

Other Books in the Night Heroes Series

Cry from the Coal Mine (Vol 1)
Free Fall (Vol 2)
Broken Brotherhood (Vol 3)
The Blade of Black Crow (Vol 4)
Ghost Ship (Vol 5)
When Serpents Rise (Vol 6)
Moth Man (Vol 7)
Runaway (Vol 8)
Terror by Day (Vol 9)
Winter Wolf (Vol 10)
Desert Heat (Vol 11)
Deadline (Vol 12)

Other Fiction

Zak Blue: Falcon Wing
Zak Blue: Enter the Maelstrom

Other Books by Dr. Wagner

Colossians: The Treasures of Deity
Daniel: Breathtaking
Ephesians: The Treasures of Family
Esther: Five Feasts and the Fingerprints of God
Galatians: Treasures of Liberty
Hosea: Love When It Matters Most

James: The Pen and the Plumb Line
Jonah: A Story of Greatness
Nehemiah: A Labor of Love
Philippians: The Treasures of Joy
Proverbs Vol 1: Bright Light from Dark Sayings
Proverbs Vol 2: Bright Light from Dark Sayings
The Revelation: Ready or Not
Romans: Salvation from A-Z
Ruth: Diamonds in the Darkness

Beyond the Colored Coat
From Footers to Finish Nails
Learning Not to Fear the Old Testament
Marriage Makers/Marriage Breakers
I'm Saved! Now What???
Don't Muzzle the Ox
Why Christmas?

Devotionals

DO Drops Vol. 1
DO Drops Vol. 2
DO Drops Vol. 3
DO Drops Vol. 4
DO Drops Vol. 5
DO Drops Vol. 6
DO Drops Vol. 7
DO Drops Vol. 8

DO Drops Vol. 9
DO Drops Vol 10
DO Drops Vol 11
DO Drops Vol 12